# Yamp

By Lyle Hill
©2021

Yampy

First paperback edition December 2021.

ISBN 9798772511565

Contact author Lyle Hill on www.facebook.com

Dedicated to Johnny Carrabin.

# 1

Even the spiders looked cold.

I know I was.

My office was a leaking armpit of a place, above a shop on the Alcester Road.

The windows didn't lock, and I didn't have the know-how or money to get them fixed. Whenever the wind caught them, they flew open, letting the rain and local glue-heads on in.

(This was perfect for a Private Investigator who had all sorts of sensitive information lying about the place.)

The wallpaper was peeling, the wiring was bad, and the mould was spreading (even *into me* it felt like - especially on hungover mornings).

The blokes who owned the shop below were okay. However, I had suspicions that they sold crack cocaine to the growing vagrant population which seemed to gestate outside.

But more than any of it, more than the damn glue-head burglars, it was the spiders that pissed me off most of all.

They were my own personal plague, sent down to torment me and only me.

Those eight-legged bastards could have split anytime they wanted. (I envied them.) But they didn't. (So, I hated them.)

Man, I'd give anything to *just leave!*

I'd live in a corner and eat flies for the rest of my life, if it meant I could split.

"This place is like a fridge!" I shouted. "And if you don't like it, then leave!" I carried on with the spiders. "You want to hear something funny? Do you? I pay money to rent this place. Can you believe that shite? I actually *pay* to be here..."

I awaited some kind of acknowledgment or response, but nothing arrived. Beady eyes just continued looking at me - mocking me.

Enough was enough.

I stood up from the desk.

A quick one-two was all it took, and the spiders were no more.

The office, however, was still like a fridge - and not a good one. No cold cuts, no chilled tins of Holsten Pils, no nothing! Just judgmental fucking spiders.

Sitting back down I wiped the spiders' entrails on my jeans. (Always jeans. Wrangler. Larstons. True class.) And when I glanced back at the wall, I watched their long legs slowly stop twitching. Their bodies were mushed into the mouldy wallpaper, and I felt good about myself.

But my one knuckle was hurting.

I never was a good puncher. I'd always relied on weapons in my times of grief. My knuckles were too sharp and my bones were too weak. But I was cunning and cruel when I wanted to be, and that always trumped any skilled boxer or grappler.

Arachnids dealt with, I leant back.

I grabbed the latest tin of Holsten from the desk and gave it a shake:

Yeah -

Empty.

Typical.

My eyes shut into beautiful darkness and from outside the broken windows I listened to life pass me by...

Engines and muffled radios, shouting, shoes slapping the pavement, birds praying for scraps, and in the back of my mind - me praying for work.

My name was Paddy Hassle -

Private Investigator.

Moseley was my turf, but Birmingham, in all its barbaric brilliance, had a way of dragging me all over. From one skid row to the next.

Moseley was an okay place.

(Well, it ought to be. I'd called it my home for long enough.)

To many, the area was chic - overrun with struggling musicians come dope-addicts, socialist painters, communist potters, etc.

I never jived with those cats. I didn't like their beards or their hemp or the bullshit that spilt out of their mouths after too many guest ales in The Prince. The Prince was the hip pub in the area. The patrons there ate kale daily and voted red. It wasn't my scene. (I liked to drink and decay in The Elizabeth of York – but we'll get to her later.)

They knew me in the pubs as Hassle. Because boy, in Moseley, or anywhere else for that matter, hassle was all I got.

I suppose being a Private Investigator sounds cool to you, right?

Well, it might be.

In Los Angeles, or fuck it, even that hellhole London.

But not in Birmingham and not in Moseley.

Oh no, no, no. It was a terrible fucking job. (I mean, you've just met me, right? Take note... the manure-pile of an office, the spider infestation and the shellshocked brain it's all given me.)

Moseley was no place to be a P.I.

I had learnt that the hard way.

*Syria or Mogadishu... any European country! Anywhere but here!*

It was the tedium that broke you down. The shouting, shagging stupidity of the local maniacs. From the glue-heads that hung around the square, to the insecure tossers who suspected their insecure tosser partners of various deviances. They were all maniacs! And now I was one of them.

In booze-hungry desperation, I snatched the can and shook it again. I was praying for a dribble, praying for a droplet of salvation. What Christ's blood did for the old bags at mass, Holsten did for me every morning.

*Fuck the work! Gimmie a drink!*

I drained the final few millilitres but could only taste tin.

Then I exhaled loudly.

I exhaled loudly because I could.

"This is my life," I said and shut my eyes again.

In the darkness, I flipped the stereo on beside my desk.

*(The Kinks, Set Me Free, 1965)*

"This is my life..." I repeated again, for any spider that hadn't heard me. "And it'll have to do."

## 2

My phone was ringing.

I must have fallen asleep because the ringtone made me jump.

Before I answered, I looked outside. The sky was grimmer somehow, greyer, and full of rain.

The stereo had turned itself off, as it was in the habit of doing. But that didn't concern me. The ringing phone did.

I wiped my eyes and grabbed it.

Recently I had changed my ringtone to the theme music from *Friday 13th (1980)*. I liked the film and I liked the theme, but it did attract some strange looks in the Co-op queue, or standing at the urinals in The Elizabeth.

(Before *Friday 13th*, I had had a tune by Karu Abe, a Japanese heroin-addicted saxophonist that I found highly amusing.)

Anyway, back to the phone –

The number was unknown, but I was used to that.

I answered it anyway.

"Yeah, what?"

"Is this Miss Hassle?"

"What?"

"Sorry, I mean – is this Mr Hassle?"

The voice was uneasy as it whispered down the line.

"Well, who is this?" I asked.

"This is John Stod."

"Okay."

"Have you heard of me, Mr Hassle?"

"No, I haven't heard of you."

"Are you sure, Mr Hassle?"

"Not really. I suffer from blackouts."

*"Blackouts?"*

"Yes. Some alcohol related, others because of strife."

It struck me that even by this point, and even after learning their name, I couldn't tell if it was a bloke or a bird. This scared me slightly. The images in my head were disturbing –

A sexless creature, smelling like cider and urine, stumbling off the number 35 bus. Of course, the 35. Always the 35…

Jesus. I needed to stop.

Then I realised we were both in silence. Not talking. Just listening to each other breathe.

Until the voice spoke again –

"So, you are unsure whether you know me or not, Mr Hassle?"

"As I said – I have blackouts. Also, my office was recently broken into by glue-heads. They stole some papers. I may have met you before, but now have no record. What was your name again? Rod? John Rod? Are you the man who broke into Sainsburys? The one who stole all those legs of lamb?"

"No, I am not, Mr Hassle."

"In that case, what can I do for you, Mr…?"

(I had already forgotten his name.)

"STOD!" The voice spoke up and confirmed it was indeed a man (or at least mostly male).

Then suddenly Stod began gasping. Gasping like –

*"Huuuuuu!*

*Haaaaaaa!"*

Like he'd suddenly recalled some impending doom.

"Mr Hassle! Oh, Mr Hassle! I must see you! I MUST! I MUST!"

Jesus Christ, the man sounded completely insane.

"Calm down, Stod. Now what's wrong?"

"Not over the phone, Mr Hassle. But please… *I must see you!"*

There was desperation in his voice – crazy, pathetic desperation. I didn't like it. It unnerved me. He sounded like a fruit. Had I spoken to this crazy, desperate fruit in The Prince some time? Had he tracked me down because he wanted to do *god-knows-what* to me? The idea was terrifying. My hands grew clammy. The phone started to slip...

"Where are you situated?" Stod asked.

His voice sounded like a prepubescent boy with hay fever.

I didn't know how to answer.

"Sir, I am not gay!" I said.

He didn't respond.

I could only hear his breathing down the phone. It seemed like he too did not know how to respond.

"Yes, right, okay, Mr Hassle. But where are you situated?"

Then it hit me –

*Keep it professional, Hassle!*

*You need the work!*

*Buggerer or not, his money is still green!*

I gave him the address and told him to look out for the sign.

"Sign?" Stod asked, confused.

"Yeah. This local kid made it for me. It's all fucked-up, but he's not the full ticket."

*"Full ticket?"*

"He's not all there."

*"All where?"*

"Listen here you idiot, I'm trying to say that the sign is all fucked-up. You'll know it when you see it. It says *Investigate Privates* or something."

"Oh my."

"I'll take it down one day, I suppose. Just not yet."

By now the fear of a possible rape had left me. I was becoming increasingly bored and restless. I wanted a drink. I wanted to get off the phone with this strange, irritating man.

I sighed.

I sighed loud.

I wanted Stod to hear me sigh and get the fucking message.

The tin of Holsten was still on my desk.

Still empty –

Still distressing me –

But it had my attention.

(More than Stod, anyway.)

"Very well, Mr Hassle, but before I decide to attend your place of business, I would like you to elucidate upon your specific strengths. If I am to trust you with my personal information, I need to know without a shadow-of-doubt that you, sir, are not only competent but -,"

I hung up the phone and leant back in the chair.

*Fuck that!*

It was then that I noticed three new spiders had crawled out onto the wall.

Were they here to mock me too?

Or had they arrived for revenge?

The only thing I could be sure of was that I needed a drink.

There was no way I would survive a meeting with John Stod if I was sober.

No way.

# 3

He looked exactly how he sounded –

Like a leaking bag of dog shit.

He had buzzed up for me and I didn't bother looking out the window before I let him in. What would be the point? I didn't know what he looked like. Just another dipshit pressing a buzzer.

(Well, maybe if he did resemble the 35-hoppin', piss-stained transvestite I would have had second thoughts. But I was skint and I needed money.)

When Stod walked in he extended a small, effeminate hand in my direction.

"Sit down, will you?" I shook my head and ignored his hand.

(Never trust a man with small hands. Never. There is a reason they have small hands. They are idle, devious and perverted. *Beware of men with small hands!*)

"Mr Hassle, thank you for meeting with me."

"Yes," I said.

I quickly (but far too late) tried to hide five empty cans of Holsten that I had consumed over the past hour. They were cluttering the desk and made me appear slightly unprofessional.

I knocked the last one over by accident, but it was half-full.

It spilt all over my laptop. The screen flashed. A motor inside rushed and then died.

I cursed myself but tried to downplay it.

"Oh my! Your laptop, Mr Hassle!" Stod said and pointed.

"Please," I raised a hand. "Please be quiet."

"But Mr Hassle, I -,"

I raised my hand higher, and he shut up.

Then I lit a Chesterfield from the pack on the desk.

I puffed it once –

Twice –

Three times –

"Mr Hassle, I need your help," Stod eventually said.

"Very well. I have some immediate questions I need to ask."

"Oh, Mr Hassle, please let me explain!"

"No need, Mr Stod," I raised my hand again and sensed his dick shrivel. "I can tell from your blatant homosexuality that you are involved in the theatre, or some other, erm, gay job. From your small, girlish hands I assume you played poorly at all sports at school. Thus, you were terribly bullied by the stronger, better children. Thus, you have tried to seek out a strong, masculine man for a partner. Correct? You also seem uneasy in the presence of an authority figure - such as myself. This is because your problem actually transcends the legal. The fact you have visited me on a weekday suggests you have no job or a very ridiculous and irrelevant one. I can tell from your sweaty hands and dishevelled appearance that you are into drugs – probably through your masculine lover. Painkillers, I believe. Tramadol, is it? Maybe originally taken for rectal pain? This, and only this, I do not know..."

I took a puff on the Chesterfield, marvelling at my own brilliance.

"Mr Stod, you are here because your masculine, drug-abusing gay lover is being unfaithful. He is either stealing money from you to fund his habit or is seeing another man who will fund it for him. Now..."

I opened the desk draw and grabbed a pen.

Blue-tipped.

Berol.

Two for three quid in Sainsburys.

The best.

"Tell me his name and address, Mr Stod. I assume..." I paused and chuckled to myself. "*Assume?* Ha-ha, how silly of me. I mean, *I know* that he does not live with you, does he? No, no, no. That is so his deviousness can persist. This *living apart* has been a matter of concern for you from the beginning, has it not?"

I looked up from the pen and through the cigarette smoke –

I saw Stod's expression -

He looked shocked.

Shocked at the ease at which I had delved into his life and found his problem?

Or – maybe – possibly – shocked for another reason?

"Mr Hassle, I don't know what to say..." he said.

"Just give me his name and address, sweetheart."

"Mr Hassle, I -,"

"We don't have much time, Mr Stod!"

"Mr Hassle, I am a music producer. I am a very important music producer!"

I paused for a moment. "No, you aren't."

"But I am, Mr Hassle!"

"Well..." I thought for a moment. "That could be considered a *gay job.*"

"AND I AM NOT GAY, MR HASSLE!" Stod suddenly screamed.

I paused again. "Yes, you are."

"NO, I AM NOT!"

"Are you sure?"

"YES, MR HASSLE! I AM SURE!"

I put the Berol away. "Very well, then please explain."

Stod sighed and rubbed at his face. "Mr Hassle, I suspect that my wife is being unfaithful."

A-ha!

"Mr Stod, did your wife, for the sake of political correctness, once have a John Thomas?"

"NO, SHE DID NOT!"

"Was she born with both a -,"

"Oh, Mr Hassle, please listen!"

"Does she wear men's -,"

"MR HASSLE!" Stod banged his fist on the desk.

I decided to be quiet. (Although this misunderstanding was confusing me, because technically it was impossible.)

"Mr Hassle, I am not a homosexual and my wife is a woman... very much so."

I didn't understand what he meant by *very much so*.

I just nodded.

"We have been married for just over a year, but I have grown suspicious... very much so."

The *very much so* thing was beginning to annoy me.

So I interrupted.

"What makes you suspicious, Mr Stod?"

After I asked the question, I remembered I had placed a final tin of Holsten in the desk after the buzzer had went.

I needed it.

I needed it soon.

"She works in a club – erm – a bar thingy," Stod stuttered.

"A brothel?"

"No. A club."

"Okay."

"I think she is having an affair with someone there, either a staff member or a regular customer."

"Yes, yes, Mr Stod. But *why* do you think that?"

Jesus Christ, he was driving me mad now. It seemed that this strange little man was just insecure. His conscious or unconscious mind simply couldn't comprehend that a woman would be interested in him – there had to be another motive behind it. But I didn't care. I didn't care at all. I just wanted the Holsten.

"She seems distant, Mr Hassle. She seems happy..."

"And that makes you suspicious?" I asked.

"You don't understand!" he suddenly wailed.

"Too right, I don't. What the fuck are you talking about?"

Stod didn't answer. Instead, he started weeping. Really loudly.

His moans were loud and high-pitched. He buried his face into his small hands (they barely covered his mouth).

As he continued to cry, I felt my hand levitate across to the desk draw –

Open it –

Feel around –

Feel around for something –

A cold, beautiful dampness –

The Holsten!

I slyly removed it from the desk while Stod cried.

Underneath the desk, I cracked it. It fizzed and foamed.

I sipped at it.

It was damp glory.

For a while I just sat there in silence.

I drank the beer and watched John Stod cry.

To begin with I was sneaky about it, hiding the Holsten between my legs and taking quick, rushed sips. But after a couple of minutes, I just left the beer on the table, taking long hits and pondering the strange scene unfolding in front of me.

Did he expect me to say or do something?

Well, I didn't.

After regaining his self-control, Stod explained for the next half hour or so about his suspicions. He didn't know how, why or with whom, but the-man-who-looked-like-a-leaking-bag-of-dog-shit was convinced his woman had another jockey.

He gave me her name and work address.

Then he paid a two-week advance without question.

When he left, he didn't attempt to shake hands, and that pleased me.

I relieved myself with the rest of the Holsten and a cigarette outside. I watched some tramp up the street attempt to climb the fence into a primary school. There were no kids there. Just tarmac and swings. Maybe he wanted to play on the swings? I would never know, because eventually he gave up and stumbled away, mumbling to himself and shaking his head. He paused a few feet further down the road and started rooting through a bin. What was he looking for? Bread crusts? Beer? Pornography? Again, I would never know. Because then he was gone.

I turned my attention to Mrs Stod's name and work address. I found myself transfixed by the piece of paper and what was written on it.

I didn't recognise her name.

But I did recognise the general area where she worked –

It was past Moseley. Away from the sandal-wearing leftists. In this area, people weren't left or right. They didn't have political opinions. They just smoked cocaine and murdered each other.

The area was saturated with dingy bars, drunkards and cheap drugs cut with carpet cleaner. The bouncers at the clubs were from war-torn countries and they like to kill.

*...you get the picture?*

By the time my daydream had ended, the Holsten had too.

So, I folded Stod's advance into my jacket pocket and I left.

# 4

The Proton Juara was, in my opinion, biblical.

Crafted by the greatest Malaysian engineers and first launched in 2001, the Juara packed a 1.1 litre Mitsubishi engine into a five door, six seated, front-engine, rear wheel-driven beast of a micro van. *Juara* in Malaysian translates to *champion*, which is how I felt whenever I slid onto its seductive fabric seats and gripped the premium rubber steering wheel. People kept out of the Juara's way when I drove it - it unnerved them - and rightly so.

I had always driven Juaras. I was a Juara man. Some people were Ford, VW, whatever. I was Juara.

It was parked in the carpark behind the shops.

Car thieves and smack-rats looking to score never tried anything shady with the Juara. I was unsure why. I think they feared me and what I would do to them.

When I slid onto the front seat, I felt myself immediately relax and sober up.

I drove well when I was drunk anyway, but the scent of the fabric removed any bleariness from my eyes and fogginess from my head. (I'd only had five or six beers anyway.)

I let the engine turn over and the beast, for a moment, purred to me like a kitten.

"You sure are something, baby!" I said, stroking the wheel.

I slipped her into first and backed the Juara out of the carpark.

I had to be careful, the Alcester Road was busy and the average driver in the area was beyond deranged.

My plan was to deposit Stod's advance in the bank, then drive home and walk to The Elizabeth. The carpark behind the shop backed onto the pub. It was merely seconds away. I knew the gaffer well. I drank there often. It was my local.

I'd relax, have a few drinks, ask a few questions and then head to Mrs Stod's place of work later in the day.

I knew what I was doing... Trust me!

# 5

Two hours later I was discharged from A&E.

The Juara had been involved in a massive auto wreck and was destroyed.

(I couldn't remember exactly what happened. There was a malfunction with both the brakes and the steering. I was going too fast and an elderly couple in an estate pulled out on me. It was all a blur. There was a woman on a bicycle involved as well. It was a mess.)

Ignoring hospital and police orders, I discharged myself and got a taxi to the pub.

The taxi driver was shouting at someone in a foreign language down his phone and Jesus Christ, it was hurting my soul.

I tried to stare out of the window and pay no attention – but it was hard.

I texted my Uzbekistani friend on the way. He dealt in cannabis and smuggled Protons. I asked him to sort me out another Juara and he said he would.

*What colour?* He asked.

*Beige.* I chose.

By the time I arrived at the pub, I was pissed off. I needed a Holsten.

"No tip?" the taxi driver asked after I paid.

"Buddy, you got more chance of platting piss," I said.

He didn't understand.

I walked straight inside The Elizabeth and ordered a Holsten from Apollo.

Apollo Somerfield was a six-and-a-half-foot, twenty-stone Rastafarian. He managed The Elizabeth, in a fashion.

The Elizabeth of York was part of a chain of pubs, Apollo just so happened to run it – and he ran it his way. The locals did as they were told, and although they could get rowdy, they never pushed

Apollo too far.

"How's it going, Hassle?" Apollo asked, as he handed me the pint.

"Can't talk, I'm working," I said, kissing the suds like the only true woman in my life.

"Yeah, looks like it!" he laughed and pointed at me.

I didn't understand what he meant.

Then I looked in the mirror behind the bar –

And I understood what he meant.

Jesus Christ, I looked like a tramp. I looked like an acquaintance of John Stod. And that wasn't good!

I needed to shave. I needed a haircut. I needed to gain a few pounds, maybe from a meal that wasn't liquid and hop based. I needed a tan. (Maybe I should get a spray?) There were bodies on the way to Robin Hood Crematorium that looked fresher than me. I looked like a homeless man with a brain problem. And not a good one. You know the kind? The ones that shout about the Old Testament by recycling bins in the rain. Yeah, that kind. The stone-cold demented kind. (It also didn't help that I was still covered in shattered glass and pieces of Juara from the auto wreck!)

The taste of Holsten ended my existentialist ponderings.

I glanced at Apollo.

Apart from being the manager, bartender, and bouncer, Apollo was also the entertainment.

I'm sure Head Office didn't know about his little cabaret.

(Well shit, they couldn't have done anything about it, even if they wanted to!)

I watched him put on his bass guitar and walk over to the amp that was plugged in by the television.

It was a big television, mounted on the wall for all the pub to see.

The football was on. An important game. League final.

The pub was packed. The punters were interested.

But Apollo started playing anyway -

His act was improvised, nonsensical slap-bass, in the style of Bernard Edwards of *Chic* or Larry Graham of *Sly and the Family Stone*. It sounded like the soundtrack to some awful seventies blaxploitation movie - *Funk Strangler*, or some jive-ass horror shit like that.

I hated it. I watched it every night. And every night I hated it.

People booed and Apollo ignored them. He wasn't very good, but he carried on, swinging himself to-and-fro, feeling the out of time rhythm and funking his way through…whatever it was that he was doing. What key was it in? Probably Z.

As I glugged the Holsten, a familiar looking face walked across to me. I couldn't remember his name or where I knew him from - but he definitely recognised me.

"Hassle!" he threw his arm around me.

He smelt like B.O. and failure.

"Get to fuck!" I pushed him away.

The guy was wasted.

"I need to talk, man…" he slurred.

"I'm working, piss off."

"I lost my job…"

"I don't care."

"I've got nothing, Hass!" he started to cry. "NOTHING!"

People started looking at him, then me, then *us*.

"I told you before, I don't care," I tried to shove him away.

"I've got nothing!" he wailed. "I'm just like you!"

"What?"

"I said - *I'm just like you!* No job… no bird… no life… Just a fucking piece of shit!"

"Hey, wait a minute -,"

"Oh, forget it, Hassle!" he threw his hands up in the air. "FORGET IT ALL!"

And then he walked off.

I signalled Apollo for another Holsten, so he stopped his performance. He handed his bass to a stranger who awkwardly held it for him, then he strutted across to me like Stevie Wonder high on crystal meth.

"What d'you reckon, Hassle?" he asked.

"About what?"

"The show, man. Are the people feeling it?"

I stared at him for a moment. "No, not at all. I've been telling you for years to stop this. Stop! For fuck sake, stop!"

"Ah, whatever man," he smiled, handed me my fresh Holsten and went back to the performance.

During the middle of Apollo's second set, a drunkard started neighing at him like a horse. Everyone in the pub found it hilarious and laughed. But out of nowhere, Apollo went berserk. It must have enraged him, because he belted the drunkard over the head with his wooden bass. It broke in half and split the man's head open.

Apollo dragged the lifeless body out the back of The Elizabeth.

In the alleyway, he threw the body into a sea of bin bags.

I had followed outside for a Chesterfield.

I lit it and looked at the bleeding body.

He wasn't neighing anymore, but the rats would eat tonight.

"Do you know this address?" I asked Apollo when I went back in, handing him Mrs Stod's work address.

He looked for a moment, then at me, and then a big smile spread across his lips.

"What?" I asked him.

"*This place?* You know this place."

"What are you talking about?"

"This is Legs Thirteen, brother."

My heartrate went up. I grabbed for the beer.

*Legs Thirteen?*

It was a strip-club that I frequented near town. I had been there only last weekend. In fact, I would be considered a regular (as pathetic as that was to admit). I knew the place well, which made it all the stranger that Stod's wife worked there.

That didn't seem to make any sense.

But I decided not to ask anything more of Apollo.

Instead, I went to the toilets upstairs. They smelt heavily of cannabis. I had always hated that smell. It smelt like turf. Like mowed grass that had been left to rot.

I pissed, then wetted and flattened down my greasy hair.

I decided to walk to Legs Thirteen.

I needed some fresh air. I needed to calm down and sober up. And I needed some time to think.

Most importantly, I needed to avoid that drunk who was bugging me by the bar.

I had some bad feelings in my blood, and some bad ideas in my brain to match. I was scared that I'd lose control and beat him senseless.

Then there would be two bodies lying outside.

# 6

Outside, I saw blood and fluid around the bin bags but no sign of the man.

I lit a Chesterfield and started walking to the strip club.

Looking up at the sky, I saw it was a brown Birmingham night. The smog and pollution coated the underbelly of the clouds, and the lighting from the streetlamps and high-rise flats casted an eerie tawny glow through the gloom above.

I inhaled the petrol fumes of hours before – fumes from cars full of people on their way home – to families, dinners, warmth and safety.

I spat.

I had been raised on petrol fumes.

Drunken revellers knocked into me as I walked. I could hear them cursing me from behind, calling me back, thirsty for violence. But I ignored them. I didn't have the time.

When eventually I saw the big pink letters of Legs Thirteen cutting through the night, my stomach started throbbing. There was a bad feeling inside me. Maybe it was stomach cancer? Or maybe it was a warning – a warning to not go inside.

Foolishly, I ignored it and walked on in.


I would regret that later.

# 7

Legs Thirteen looked like it always did. It was full of losers lonesomely lusting. These wasters never did anything, some didn't even pay for extras. They just sat there and watched and dreamed – maybe trying to steal a free mental image for back at their one room flats later. A couple of groups of younger men were always around, on stag-dos or just nights out.

The girls on stage were of awful quality. I saw visible eczema and C-section scars. I wouldn't recommend it.

I walked across to the bar and the barmaid recognised me.

I didn't have to ask -

The Holsten was on its way.

I was nervous for some reason. Maybe I was coming down off the booze high from The Elizabeth. Or maybe it was because I was working. I didn't know. All I did know was that the strange feeling in my gut from outside had followed me inside too.

I paid the barmaid without a word between us. I knew the price.

An instinct was telling me not to ask her about Mrs Stod –

But I asked anyway.

"Excuse me!" I shouted.

*Stone In Love* by *Journey* was playing loud.

On stage, an overweight blond with hair like hay was throwing herself round a rusty pole. She had bruises on her thighs. The crowd loved it.

"Yes?" the barmaid asked me.

"I'm looking for someone."

"Isn't everybody in here?"

"No, not like that."

She paused. *"Not like what?"*

I sighed deeply. "You know…"

I said it threateningly without meaning to.

She stared at me like I was scaring the shit out of her.

"I'm not sure I know what you're talking about," she said.

"Listen here, babe, let me do the talking, capeesh?"

Now she looked annoyed. "Sir, how can I help?"

"I'll get to that in a second."

"Please! Please! What do you want?"

I handed her the piece of paper that Stod had given me.

She looked at it for moment. Then she looked at me. Then back at the paper. Then back at me. Then at a drunk leaning up the bar. Then back at me again. I was about to lose it, big time, OJ-style.

"What d'you want her for?" she eventually asked.

"Just a couple of questions. Nothing heavy."

She considered me for a moment –

Was I a foaming-mouthed sex psycho?

Was I a murderous ex?

I must have looked like neither –

Just a loser with a couple of questions.

"She's due on shift in a minute," she said quickly. "You'll have to wait."

She put the paper down on the bar and walked off.

I tried to say *thanks*, but she was already gone.

Instead, I sipped the Holsten.

While I waited, I thought about some things. I wondered why Stod's wife worked the bar in such a dump. If he really was an important music producer like he said, then she didn't have to work, let alone in such a hole. It bugged me. Something wasn't adding up. Yet, I had no idea *just how much* things wouldn't add up –

"Hey babe, are you playing me?" I shouted to the barmaid over *Dreaming* by *Blondie*.

"No, I will not!" she shouted back.

"What?"

"I will not play with you!"

"No. I said, were you *playing* me?"

She didn't understand. She left the pint she was pouring and walked over to me. (I got the vibe I was becoming a problem customer.)

"What now?" she huffed.

"Well, where the fuck is she then?"

"Eyes to the stage, moron! She's been on for ten minutes!"

*Eyes to the stage?*

I turned.

And laid my eyes on Mrs Stod...

She looked nothing like I imagined. She had natural red hair that burnt like wildfire as she moved. There was something both majestic and deadly about her at the same time. I thought of a cobra gliding through sands, or a shark glimmering below blue waters. She had curves in all the right places. In an instant I knew she was perfection.

How long did she dance? Ten minutes? Ten hours? I didn't know.

I was in a void.

(Holsten no longer interested me.)

When the show finished, I downed the remains of my pint and rushed across to her. I needed to speak to her. I decided that if I asked for a private show in the back room, then I would have my opportunity.

She was strutting through the locals and newcomers alike when I got to her. Both groups were grabbing out at her brilliance with eager faces, boyish eyes and handfuls of cash.

When Mrs Stod saw me, her face changed. I didn't give her time to think. I just slammed a oner into her open hand and saw in her face that she agreed.

"In the back," she said.

"I'm not into that. Just a dance for now."

She didn't laugh at my joke.

"Hey, pal!" a little old man said and tapped me. "You haven't got the right!" He had a crumpled fiver in his wrinkly old hand.

"Scram!" I shoved him, not hard, but either way he went staggering backwards like a newborn calf and bashed into a table, knocking over some drinks.

I walked quickly with Mrs Stod and could hear shouting and scuffling behind me.

As I shut the private room door behind me, I felt like a god. I sneered at all the jealous faces that were still watching me with her. But when I turned to face Mrs Stod – I was wearing a scowl.

My fists were clenched.

And my father was pouring out of me, once again.

"WHAT THE FUCK IS GOING ON?" I shouted at her.

She jumped. "Jesus, what's wrong, Paddy?"

I grabbed her arm and led her further into the room, away from the door and any nosy perverts that might have been listening. "Your husband turned up at the office today."

*"What?"* she gasped.

"He asked me to look into you!"

Whatever sexiness she was trying to convey fell from her flesh in an instant. She slumped forwards into a slight hunch and her face ran pale. "What do you mean?"

"Are you hard of hearing?" I grunted. "John Stod called me up. He reckons *his wife* is being unfaithful. He gave me your name and work address. He also gave me a two-week advance!" I patted the cash under my jacket.

"Shit! Shit! Shit!" Mrs Stod pulled on a silk robe from a hanger on the wall and started pacing around.

"Does he know about me?" I asked.

"Well, he must be suspicious!"

"No shit. But how? We've been careful."

"I don't know, Paddy! He's got eyes everywhere."

"Who, *Stod?!*"

"Don't underestimate him. He's a powerful man."

"I'm real scared."

"Look…" she got up close to me. She smelt good. "Drop the hard-man act, because this is both of our futures on the line, okay?"

"*My future?* How did you work that out?"

"Like I said… don't underestimate him."

For a few moments we both worried in silence. We shared our concerns without speaking.

I had been shagging Mrs Stod for about two months. I didn't know her name. I didn't bother asking and she didn't seem to care. For some reason, this red-headed-ten had taken a liking to me. She'd given me a private show and before I knew it, I was buying her drinks after her shift. I put it down to my quick wit and thick fringe. By the end of the night, she was jumping on top of me on the fold-out bed back at the office. We put on some show for the spiders that night. It really was something. And the one-night fling turned into a weekly occurrence. I looked forwards to them. But I was stupid. I should have done my research and taken my time. A thing too good to be true usually is, and the cheapest bird usually costs the most. Just like an Irish welder once told me: *There isn't enough blood in a man's body to run the brain and the dick!*

"We need to stop this," she said suddenly, shaking her head.

Something winded me, like a left hook to the solar plexus –

Fear.

"Don't overreact!" I said.

"I can't fuck this up, Paddy. I can't! I've spent too many years bumming around – too many wankers – all of them treating me like shit. I'm not going back to drunks and estates, no way. John treats me good. I don't love him, but he treats me good. The house is nice too. But I'm safe - I'm finally safe!"

"But…" I stopped before I embarrassed myself. I had a quick think and changed what I was going to say: "But that'll look suspicious. Changing from being out every weekend to suddenly the perfect housewife? The little shitheel will know something's up. If he's as slick as you say he is, you've got to carry on like everything is normal, like there's nothing for you to get caught at, that you're not doing anything wrong." I took a breath. "We've got to play our cards right, babe."

"So, what do we do then?" she was looking into my eyes, she was totally vulnerable, and in that fragment of a moment - she was all mine.

"We need to be more careful. *You* need to be more careful."

"What does that mean, Paddy?"

"It means, well, when was the last time you shagged him?"

Mrs Stod turned red in the cheeks. They matched her hair. "None of your business!"

"Listen, cook him a pie or beat him off. Something! Something to show you care - to show you're happy - to show that you're not messing around!"

She shrugged. She looked like she was going to cry. "But I'm not happy and I don't care."

I didn't know what to say -

So, I said something stupid -

"Leave him then."

"I can't."

"Why not?"

*Shut up, Hassle. You're showing her your hand!*

"He looks after me. I'm safe!"

"Darling," I held her gently by both shoulders, she was trembling. "If *this* is happening now, then *this* will happen again too. With me, or without me."

"What do you mean?" she whimpered, wiping a tear from her eye.

"You're on borrowed time. Sometimes you've got to call it a day. To know when you're beat. You had a good thing going, but it's run its course."

She didn't say anything.

She knew I was right but didn't want to admit it.

"I'll be seeing you," I said and planted a kiss on her forehead. Then I left.

# 8

Outside Legs Thirteen, I felt pissed off. I liked the nameless girl, Mrs Stod, and I didn't want to lose her. It wasn't just the sex. She was sweet and crazy in all the right ways. As I walked, I wondered what would happen. Would she run away? Would she leave the club? If she quit, then I'd never see her again. I didn't know where she or Stod lived. That would be the end of us. I hoped she wouldn't, but I knew there was a possibility she might.

"Don't do it, darling..." I whispered to an alleyway that I walked past.

The night was dark and the roads were full of fog.

I could hear footsteps behind me.

It sounded like they were trying to walk in-time with mine. This sent alarm bells ringing. An old mugger's trick – walk in time with the victim so they'd don't hear you creeping up.

As I began to turn, the footsteps broke into running –

The Holsten must have slowed me down, because by the time I turned to face my foe an iron bar was already crunching into the bridge of my nose.

I didn't remember falling –

But suddenly I was looking up at the night sky.

Everything was quiet.

Slow... Blurry... Dull...

Like the universe had just spiked a vein.

Voices were talking among themselves, but I couldn't hear what they were saying...

I rolled onto my front and touched my face. My nose felt like a lump of raw chicken breast. I couldn't make out skin or bone or anything. It was all numb, and it didn't feel like *my face* anymore.

As my vision returned, I watched blood pooling on the pavement slab below my face.

Suddenly someone grabbed my legs.

They started dragging me backwards towards the alleyway, and then down into it.

On the way, I lost control of my bladder.

I heard muffled laughter from my attackers and then one of them kicked me in the bollocks.

"CUNTS!" I gargled through the blood and snot that was gathering in my mouth.

I felt a hand go into my jean pocket and start feeling around. Then it started checking the other ones. I tried to swat it away feebly, but it did no good. Then the hand reached into my jacket pocket and found Stod's advance. The advance I never managed to deposit into the bank!

For a moment I tried to concentrate through the blurriness and the blood -

I saw a callused, white hand with a swallow bird tattoo just above the thumb -

(I stored that image in my long-term memory.)

Just lying there and letting those bastards take my money made me feel pathetic. But what could I do? I was drunk and delirious. If I tried to fight back, I could have been killed.

Footsteps and laughter echoed as my attackers disappeared.

They would disappear to spend my money on drugs or look for other drunken victims around Birmingham's city centre.

My face was swelling by the second.

Lumps were creeping into my vision.

I was almost blind.

I couldn't be bothered to move. I just lay still, in the urine and the blood, and let warm unconsciousness take me away from the pain.

My last thoughts were about Mrs Stod:

*"Don't do it, darling..."*

# 9

I was discharged from hospital the next morning and I felt feral.

I glared at anyone who looked at my swollen face, and I didn't drink. I never touched alcohol when I was angry (at least to begin with) – it blunted my edge.

My father was oozing through me again like a septic puss. He oozed through me in every single negative trait – anger, disgust, sloth, addiction. I even heard myself say: *Tae fuck with ya!* When a taxi ignored my extended arm.

"Enough," I said to myself, shaking the horrible old bastard from my bones and reverting back to Hassle.

A nurse had told me that I'd been found by PCSOs in the alleyway.

At some point during the night, homeless people had stolen my jeans. The PCSOs thought they'd stumbled across a rape victim to begin with. I didn't know why the nurse felt the need to share this with me, but she did, in depth.

After waiting for about an hour for a taxi driver who was brave, or dumb enough to pick me up, I was eventually on my way home.

He kept asking about my face.

"Why them do that to you?" he kept repeating.

"I was mugged."

"I think maybe. But why them do that?"

I couldn't understand what he meant. Instead, I just stared out the window at Birmingham in the rain. Birmingham suited the rain. It needed it. It suited overcast, grey days that melted into nothing. Mondays that crawled into Tuesdays. Saturdays that became Sundays, and then limped on into a new week. Seven-day-weekends. But poor, empty weekends with nothing to do, no money to spend, no friends to visit or life to lead. I didn't know what day it was. I didn't care. Time and days no longer applied to me. I was infinite.

Finally back in Moseley, I walked into the carpark around the back of the shop.

My new Proton Juara had arrived.

But someone had broken into the back and shit all over the seats.

"TAE FUCK WITH YA!" I roared, before spotting a police car parked several feet away.

A copper got out and approached me.

He explained that he had arrived after reports of a vandalised vehicle, possibly dumped.

I already hated him. He seemed staunchly Protestant and with a serious BTK-vibe. A straight-shooter. A jogger. A healthy-eater. A wanker. The kind of wanker who pissed clear.

"Yes, this is mine," I told him and signalled at the car.

"What happened to your face?" he asked.

*Think fast, Hassle!*

"Rogue waves," I said.

The copper seemed confused, so I carried on quickly –

"The car? The car?"

"Yes sir, very peculiar indeed," he began pacing around it.

"What do you mean?" I peered into the back and nearly vomited from the smell of fresh shit.

"I mean, the abnormally large amount of human waste. I've seen this before – revenge defecation – but not on this level. There must have been multiple excreters."

"I'd like to think so."

"Would you consider yourself an unpopular man, Mr Hassle?"

I thought for a second. "I'm not sure," I lied.

"Right then, please wait here. You have to sign an incident report."

"OH, FUCKING HELL!"

As the copper walked back to his car, I waited impatiently.

I don't know why I did it –

But I released the boot hatch from beside the steering wheel.

Then I walked round the back –

Opened it up –

And looked inside –

A strong, grassy smell hit me at the back of the nostrils.

"What now?" I moaned to myself. "Has someone filled the boot with some kind of shrubbery?"

The smell was familiar –

Rotting turf...

It was a brick of cannabis!

A big one. Neatly wrapped and placed perfectly on top of the spare wheel.

"Shit."

I looked up and saw the copper was already walking back to me.

I tried to meet him half-way.

"Very well, very well. Is that what I have to sign?" I smiled through the swelling and pointed at the paper in his hand.

"You *will*."

"Why did you say it like that?" I asked.

"Like what?"

"*Will*... You said it strangely."

"Because I have to complete the search. I need to check the interior of the automobile, glove compartment and boot. You needed to be present for this. If all is well, then you are free to go and the vehicle is yours."

He smiled at me like a sadist at Belsen. He enjoyed his power over little men like me. He probably went home and pleasured himself over the thought of it. Power is one thing. Some people are born into power – they have no choice – they are natural leaders, natural thinkers. They have power because people follow them and respect them. They have not chosen it and did not seek it. But the truly evil, twisted bastards of the world are those who *long* for power, *strive* for it and need it like novocaine before surgery. They are the people to watch. They are the people with skeletons in their closets, bad things on their internet histories and foul intentions in their minds. And this copper… he was definitely one of them.

He started poking around inside the car, and I half respected him for even wanting to.

But I needed to think fast.

If – no - *when* he checked the boot, he would find the cannabis.

Then I would be in deep shit…

Even deeper shit than my back seats!

Using my cunningness, I thought quickly and then spotted my saving grace:

A fat man on crutches was struggling his way across the carpark. He was wearing an Angela Lansbury *Murder She Wrote* t-shirt for some reason, and he looked close to the end.

My plan came together.

While the copper was preoccupied inside the car, I grabbed a piece of broken brick from a nearby crumbling wall.

Then I threw it at the disabled man.

It sailed over the car, over the oblivious policeman's head, over the tarmac, through the air… and straight into the man's face.

"AHHHHHHHHH!" he screamed like he was being savaged by dogs.

(At school I had been terrible at P.E. I was always picked last at team sports. *Always.* We had an African boy in our class who had rickets. And I was even picked after him. But the throw I performed that day – with such velocity and accuracy – made up for all those years of embarrassment at school.)

The copper looked up, startled, just in time to see the fat disabled man fall onto a grit bin.

The grit bin collapsed under his weight and the fat disabled man rolled onto the floor, covered in road grit.

"Good god!" the copper exclaimed, abandoning his search and rushing over to help.

"Me cowin' face is bost!" I could hear the fat man say.

I wanted to watch the copper attempt to lift him, but I had no time.

Working fast, I opened the boot and grabbed the brick of weed.

I looked up –

The fat man was back on his feet –

And the copper was looking right at me!

SHIT!

I turned and blindly hurled the weed as hard as I could -

But I had forgotten the police car was parked directly behind me -

The brick of cannabis hit straight into the windscreen –

It exploded –

Sending lumps of weed flying in all directions –

It was like a drizzle in hippie heaven.

*Good one, Hassle...*

"WHAT IS THAT?" the copper demanded as he rushed over.

"What is what?"

"THAT!"

He pointed at the weed all over his car and the ground, some bits still fluttering through the air.

"Look, I don't know."

"That is drugs!"

"Is it? I don't know."

"Are they your drugs?"

"Absolutely not!"

"Explain yourself!"

"Explain what?"

"YOURSELF!" Spittle was bubbling at the sides of his mouth, and a vein was pulsating in his forehead.

"Listen, buddy. That's there, and I'm here. What's your point?"

"That is an awful excuse!"

"I don't need an excuse. Whatever *that is,* it's over there. I'm stood here. Do you understand?"

"I saw you."

"Saw me?"

"Yes."

"Saw me, what?"

He didn't say another word. He just stood there – like water boiling in a pan. He was furious. He wanted to hurt me.

"But one thing I will say…" I finally broke the silence. "Your pals are going to laugh their bollocks off when you bring that car back." He turned and looked at it. "You got a nickname at the station yet? Because I reckon it'll be Detective Doobymobile."

I don't think he understood what I said.

And I hadn't exactly said what I wanted to say.

But the general message of – *you'll do yourself more harm than good by arresting me* – seemed to immediately sink in.

Without another word, he handed me the piece of paper. I signed it. Then he took it back and walked over to his car, dusting off the lumps of cannabis.

I tried not to push my luck, so I quickly scaled the back stairs from the carpark up to my office.

There were tins of Holsten up there.

But I wouldn't be drinking them.

I needed to stay mad.

# 10

It wasn't even noon and I was ready for bed. Ready for sickness. Ready for death.

But instead of dying, I lit a Chesterfield and started thinking about my dilemma. (Or should I say, *dilemmas?*)

My Uzbekistani friend refused to accept responsibility for the cannabis. He said it wasn't his and he didn't touch the stuff anymore... but of course he would say that.

By the end of our texting conversation, I just didn't care.

I just wanted the car cleaned and repaired, and he said he would.

He was a good guy really – just ex-Soviet and deranged.

To relax, I played some *Electric Prunes* and hummed along.

I was becoming obsessed with murdering my muggers. I wanted to punish them for what they had done to me. The doctor had had to reset my nose. It had been flattened into my face and my right cheekbone was fractured also. All-in-all, I was a mess. I finally looked how I felt. My face looked like a Halloween pumpkin in mid-November, disfigured and deformed. They'd had to drain the fluid and prescribe me anti-inflammatories to reduce the swelling and the likelihood of piss-taking in pubs.

At my feet, underneath the desk, was Putlog.

I should have taken him with me last night, I thought.

(Then again, I was too drunk for him to have been any use!)

Putlog was a three-foot scaffold tube. He was aluminium. You could get steel tubes, but steel was too slow and too heavy. Ally was quicker and lighter. Yes, less damage. But trust me, you wouldn't want to be hit by *either* of them.

My favourite trick with Putlog was to tape him to the outside of my forearm, running down from elbow to wrist. When I pulled my leather jacket over the top, you couldn't tell he was there.

I had perfected the forearm smash technique. So when I swung my forearm into your face, it was Putlog that was doing the kissing...

Chin –

Jaw –

Forehead –

Temple –

Even throat, one time –

Past experience had proven that it didn't matter where exactly I landed...

They always went down.

"Mr Hassle!"

I awoke from my daydream and span around in the chair.

The last person on earth that I wanted to see, was letting himself in -

John Stod looked nervous and sweaty. He walked across the office floor and took a seat without being invited to.

"You've got the timing of a stroke. D'you know that, Stod?"

He ignored me.

"What happened to your face, Mr Hassle?" Stod asked.

"What d'you mean?"

"The swelling and the bruising?"

"What swelling? What bruising?"

He got the message. He shut up and averted his eyes.

Then Stod coughed and tried to remember what reason he'd came to see me.

"Just a scuffle..." I mumbled under my breath. "Nothing to worry about."

"Mr Hassle, I thought I would bring you some information," Stod started poking around inside his caramel-coloured jacket.

"Oh yes?"

"Yes. I believe I may have a suspect."

"A suspect?"

"Yes. Someone who may be having relations with my wife."

My knee started jittering.

I was nervous.

I half expected him to produce a picture of me. A picture of me, with my address written below. But then I realised that would have been absurd.

*What then?*

I was panicking.

Afterall, it was *me* who was shagging his wife. It was *me* that he was paying to find.

I was chasing myself – and being paid to do it!

"This... This..." Stod began to descend into some kind of enraged trance. "This... THIS..." His volume increased as he removed a crumpled picture from his pocket. "THIS FRICKING IDIOT!"

He handed it to me, and I unfolded it.

Through the lumps in my vision, I saw the image of a dead body lying in a swamp.

"What?" I was confused.

"I believe it to be him," Stod nodded.

"What? This corpse?" I looked again – yes, it was definitely dead. "What are you saying? She is some sort of necrophile?"

"No, Mr Hassle!" Stod stood up and pointed at the picture in my hand. "This man is alive!"

I looked once more:

The emaciated meth-head in the picture was allegedly alive, although I would have bet money that he wasn't. Whoever he was, he must have weighed about eight-stone soaking wet. I could see his skull through the lack of skin on his head. His hair was dyed an awful blue colour and his spread-eagle arms were cluttered with scabs and needle marks. I was repulsed.

"*This?* This is the man your wife is fucking?"

Stod shuddered as I said those words. "I believe so."

"Who is it?" I asked, still convinced he was dead.

"His name is Val Vulva. He plays lead guitar for The Gulldongs."

"Oh really?" I shot him a smile and started rocking in my chair.

"The Gulldongs, you say? I have all their records."

"You do?"

Then I snapped –

"NO, OF-COURSE-FUCKING-NOT! What are you talking about? You've turned up here, uninvited, sweating and looking like shit. Then you hand me this picture of a half-rotten corpse in a swamp and start yammering on about vulvas and gongs. Are you on medication? Are you missing from a facility somewhere? Because you creep the shit out of me, Stod!"

Stod was flummoxed. "I didn't mean to offend you, Mr Hassle. I just -,"

"ENOUGH! ENOUGH!" I didn't know what I was mad about yet, I just knew I was mad. "ENOUGH!" I started banging my fist on the desk. "Enough with this *Mr Hassle* bollocks. Even the priests and the imams round here call me shithead!"

"Val Vulva is a regular at my wife's work!" Stod tried to argue.

"And so are a million other pricks. So why him? Because of his toilet duck coloured hair?"

"He is an up-and-coming star! His band The Gulldongs are set to sign a big record deal, Mr Hassle. I suppose, maybe, she saw him as a means to escape. He offered her a ticket, an opportunity if you will, to not only -,"

"Ah shut up."

I was craving a Holsten now.

Sobriety gave me an edge - but fuck the edge.

Blunt me the fuck up.

I wanted to get pissed!

"Do you have an address for..." I couldn't bring myself to say it at first... "Vulva?"

"*Val* Vulva," Stod said with a stupid fucking smile on his face. "And yes, I do."

He removed another piece of paper from his jacket.

Scribbled onto it was the address of a hotel and a room number:

*Room 534, The Radison, Holloway Circus.*

I knew the joint.

It was in Birmingham city-centre.

The surrounding area was a dump, but the hotel itself was a nice place – classy, even. This surprised me. The Radison didn't strike me as the kind of place meth-heads hung out and died at.

"You shouldn't struggle to access his room," Stod continued.

"And why's that?"

He leant forward, raising a hand to the side of his mouth and whispering: "He is a dope taker."

I didn't respond. I just stared at him.

"I'll look into it," I finally said.

"Oh, thank you, Mr Hassle! Thank you, thank you!"

He stood up and walked towards the door to leave. "And I do apologise for my language earlier."

(Did he mean when he said *fricking idiot?*)

I shut my eyes and sighed.

Then I heard the door close.

I was alone again. Finally.

After a few moments, I looked at the picture of Val Vulva again, and then the address where I could find him.

The sense of déjà vu was nauseating.

I wondered what kind of fucked-up state I would return from this one in?

If I'd had any idea, then I wouldn't have gone.

# 11

After Stod left, I popped downstairs to the shop. The lads supplied me with two packs of Chesterfields. They also gave me thirteen pence off the price but seemed disappointed with my less-than-overjoyed reaction.

I went back up to the office and started chain-smoking.

After some thought, I decided that John Stod was oblivious to my involvement with his wife.

I also decided that the best course of action was to go and visit this Val Vulva. I wanted to appear busy and keep the suspicion shifted from myself. Also, as an immoral scumbag, I figured I could milk Stod a while longer.

Lead him on –

Visit Vulva –

Find some clues that lead to nowhere –

Drag it out –

More weeks –

More cash –

This was especially appealing, considering my two-week advance had been stolen, meaning that technically I was working the next fortnight for free.

Outside my office, I saw grit was still everywhere, but the Juara had vanished.

I walked across the carpark to the back entrance of The Elizabeth.

It felt like the longest walk in my life.

But I needed some Dutch courage.

My anger was already lifting, and this worried me. I knew I would get drunk at The Elizabeth. If I was truly going to burglarise Val Vulva's room, then I needed to be with-it, not a drooling idiot. But what could I do? I had to drink.

Outside The Elizabeth's back doors, I held myself back. I smoked a Chesterfield and tried to decide if it was really the best move –

passing through them – descending inside – descending, just descending in general...

I thought about Mrs Stod.

*What is going on, Hassle?* I asked myself. *Do you have feelings for this woman?*

"Fuck no!" I spluttered into the cigarette.

(A woman smoking a menthol superking glared at me. She looked like a Yorkshire ripper victim from the seventies – bad haircut and cheap, blue makeup. She looked like a miserable old bitch. Her face could have stopped a clock. But I was sure that deep down she probably wanted something dreadful to happen to her. She wanted to be on the front of the Birmingham Mail, with a stern look on her face, telling everyone how *there was nothing nobody could* do, and how *I has lost all confidence*, and how *it's really affected me mental health.*)

Anyway, back to Mrs Stod –

I wondered if she would run away with me.

Could the pair of us leave Birmingham and our crappy lives behind?

No longer would she have to shake her beautiful body for that undeserving puddle of humanity. And no longer would I have to scrape a living from other people's misfortunes. I could be happy.

But I didn't deserve happiness.

I was too much of a bastard.

Jesus, Buddah, or whatever arsehole ran the show (and some arsehole *always* runs the show), would never allow it.

Maybe Mrs Stod was involved with Val Vulva, as well as me.

Maybe Stod was right.

Maybe she was planning on disappearing with the rock star.

But would I tell Stod about it if I discovered it was true?

Would I fuck up her chances of escape, just so I could keep her a while longer?

I knew so little about myself that it scared me.

There was a stranger living inside my brain, and he was supposed to be me.

Eventually, the Chesterfield ended.

I looked through the pub doors, to what lay within –

Freedom.

Freedom from sober thought...from clarity...but mainly, from reality and all the bullshit that went along with it.

Man, I was craving a Holsten. And I was sure the German Pilsner would do more to lift my mood and reduce my swelling than any medication could.


Fuck it.

# 12

Apollo caught my eye as I entered, and he knew what to do.

I sat my arse down and waited.

A vagrant tried to enter the pub from the same door as me. He pushed even though the sign said *pull*. He pushed again. And again. Then he started screaming and ran away.

I admired Apollo's mango-coloured slacks as he strutted across the sticky carpeted floor, dumping the Holsten in front of me.

"How's it going?" he asked, combing his tumbleweed hair.

I attended to business first, then I answered. "Not bad. I'm working."

He laughed loud, really loud, like I was a complete idiot.

"You're always working, always working! You ever get any work done, Pad?" he giggled to himself as he walked away.

"How would you know?" I grumbled to myself, before attending to more business.

I watched Apollo do the empties from across the pub:

He tipped all the suds, dribbles of booze, the final bubbles of foam, gatherings of spit and saliva, from all the glasses into a big jug. Then he started wiping them. He wiped the lipstick marks, the smudges, the scum and the blood from around the edges. Patrons with dry and bleeding lips, cold sores, wounds, or internal haemorrhaging, had tainted the glasses in one way or another. (A future hepatitis outbreak with inevitable.)

When the glasses were done, he took the jug of dregs and tipped the overflow trays from beneath the taps in too. Lager, ale, stout, cider and mild – they all went in.

This jug was for Yellow Pete.

They called him Yellow Pete because he had drunk so much that his body had changed colour.

(This was probably a sign that he should cut down.)

Pete was dying slowly – the bottle saw to that. But he was also happy – the bottle saw to that too. *Happily dying a joyful death* – the demise of any true alcoholic.

I liked Yellow Pete. I liked watching him. Here was a soul more degenerate and pathetic than my own. I kept him around. By comparison then, I wasn't too bad.

I also liked how Apollo hadn't mentioned my obliterated face.

I came to the conclusion that he was probably too stoned to notice.

(Now, this may sound unbelievable, but Apollo Somerfield – the Rastafarian, slap-bass-playing pub landlord, indulged in marijuana.

[Yes, I too was shocked when I found out.]

In a rare moment of generosity, Apollo had given me one of his marijuana cigarettes, after I complained about trouble sleeping.

I smoked it there and then, out the back of The Elizabeth, by the bins.

Oh boy...

It took me all day to get home.

[Remember my office overlooked The Elizabeth? Yeah, I was that cabbaged...]

For a week after, I continually had nightmares about a plague of apes trying to kill me.

I complained to Apollo about it.

"Yeah, my shit is heavy," he'd laughed, before proceeding to describe the ingredients of *his shit*:

Cambodian mountain skunk, PCP and the finest Stechford spice.

No wonder...)

I moved from the table I was at, to a darker corner.

People came and went, but I remained where I was, sipping at pint after pint, and staring at the picture and address of one Val Vulva.

(I had been in a band once, in my youth. We were called *Sickle Cell Anaemia*. We were thrash-punk. We were young and crazy and didn't give a damn about rules, partings or slacks. I played guitar and glockenspiel and did most of the song writing. But we never

49

really took off. We played some gigs, some *major* gigs. We once headlined *Stoke Grunge Fest*, but to no success. Sickle Cell Anaemia eventually broke-up when our lead singer was arrested for trying to rob a building society with a rounder's bat. I used to email the band about a possible reunion tour, but none of the messages were ever returned...)

The drink was making me nostalgic, and I detested it.

I hated looking, thinking or talking about the past.

If anyone started a sentence with *"Remember when..."* I split.

Then, out of nowhere –

I saw my father for a moment.

I grabbed the Holsten and hit it hard.

*Forget him! Forget him!* I said to myself, trying to stop myself from shaking.

Only then did I realise it had been Yellow Pete, not the old man.

Fucking hell, he'd been dead for years...

But somehow that cunt was always nearby.

# 13

Hours rolled by, and before I knew it, the brightness outside The Elizabeth's windows grew dimmer and dimmer, draining away to nothing but darkness.

I didn't know what time it was –

But I knew it was late.

It was burglary hour.

*So, what was I waiting for?*

I stood up to go for a piss and suddenly realised just how drunk I was. Then I looked across to beside the television and spotted Apollo, mid-set. He was swinging himself to-and-fro, as he always did, and the slap-bass was sending vibrations through the floor, across the floor and into me.

Something was coming over me...

Something strange...

Something uncontrollable...

Instead of walking to the toilets, I felt myself being drawn into the centre of the room.

Eyes all around the pub fell onto the lone drunken idiot. He was preparing himself. He inhaled deeply.

Then for some reason I began performing the Cincinnati Drill.

The Cincinnati Drill was a much-revered rockn'roll dance. It involved violent ankle twists and aggressive boogieing – almost seizure-like.

In my mind I was Elvis. The King.

...but pint glasses soon started flying in my direction.

I felt cheap lager, cider (or maybe urine) begin to cover me.

Peanuts and pickled onions ricocheted off my body, but I refused to cease my performance.

Then the bastards started shrieking:

"STOP HIM! SOMEBODY STOP HIM!"

"OH, THAT VILE MAN! LOOK AT THAT VILE MAN!"

"CALL THE POLICE!"

I vaguely heard Apollo trying to calm down the agitated pub patrons across his mic. He tried his best, but this only intensified the volley of bar snacks and liquids that pasted me.

When I was ready, I finished my dance and waddled to the toilets.

I was soaked and filthy –

But I felt like I had *released something* in my performance of the Cincinnati Drill.

But what?

A deep-rooted angst?

What?

Soon I realised that what I had released - was my bladder.

I had pissed all over my best jeans, so I stuffed them into the toilet cistern and walked down into The Elizabeth's cellar in just my pants. Luckily, no one spotted me.

In the cellar, I threw my boxers away and retrieved a spare pair of jeans that I kept hidden in case of emergencies.

These came in handy, as I often somehow soiled them or tore them in knife fights (more so than other knife fighters, because I favoured a kicking-technique).

Down in the dark, alone with my humiliation and drunken mind, listening to the hustle-and-bustle of laughter and menace from above, I helped myself to a couple of bottles and wondered to myself...

*Was this it, Hassle?*

*Late thirties, alone and degenerate?*

But I couldn't be bothered to try and bleed an answer from my brain.

And then, somewhere in the blackness of the cellar, my father spoke:

"Get yer arse up, ya useless fucker, ye!"

I stood up.

"Get on with yer fucking werk!"

In a panic, I managed to find the door.

I staggered up the staircase and didn't dare look back.

Then I fell out of the pub's front door, outside, into a choking Birmingham night.

I was ready to burgle.

I had to be.

Drunken or not.

# 14

I hailed a taxi and took it to The Radison hotel. Outside, I smoked a Chesterfield and tried to ready myself for the crime I was about to commit.

Through the entrance I could see a lone receptionist at a desk. The lifts and stairs were behind her.

When I finished the cigarette I walked inside, trying to convey confidence but reeking of self-doubt (as well as possibly urine).

"Hello, may I help you?" the receptionist asked me.

*Think fast, Hassle!*

"No," I replied, and walked casually up to the lifts.

I pressed the button and waited. Without turning around, I could feel her eyes on the back of my head. She didn't say anything. And somehow that was worse.

When the lift doors opened, I darted inside and shut them behind me.

I felt safe.

But the sense of security was merely a mirage.

I shut my eyes and smelt him...

Tobacco and whiskey.

My father.

I reopened my eyes and saw him behind me in the reflection of the lift's mirror. He had been following me for a few days now. I knew an apparition was soon to occur – and now here he was.

I always recognised him instantly –

From his crooked nose, to his starch grey eyes like potato water – devoid of any life.

"What do you want?" I asked him, the same question every time, never answered, while my knees lost strength.

"I just want tae look at ye," he hissed. "The failure I raised."

His breath burnt like firewater.

And when I glanced at his jaundiced knuckles, their taste returned to my mouth.

"Just fuck off and leave me alone."

"I'll never leave ye alone, boy," he gritted his teeth. (I always knew I was getting a clout when those rotten incisors started grinding and creaking.)

"Why's that?" I started to feel brave when I remembered I was drunk. "Is hell too hot for an old mick like you? The frost and drizzle are more your cup of tea, aren't they? The same stuff that coursed through your veins."

"Smart arse," he smirked. "Just like yer mother. But it didn't do her any fucking good neither!"

"*Smart?* She married you!"

He laughed, then he repeated himself: "I'll never leave ye, boy."

"And why's that?"

"Because I'm in ye," he pointed a rheumatoid finger at me. "You are me... yer father's son."

"I'll never be like you!" I shouted back at the mirror.

He moved the finger up to his nose. "We're lookin' similar too..."

I touched mine and it was just as lumpy as his.

"I've got nothing of yours," I closed my eyes again and willed him to disappear. "Only your blood in me... and I poison that every chance I get!"

"I never loved you," I heard him whisper into my ear from the darkness.

"Good," I stuttered. "I don't know what kind of devil I would have had to be for you to love me!"

I opened my eyes –

I thought he was still stood there for a moment, still staring –

But that was me.

I was alone.

The mistake scared me – mistaking *him* for *me*.

Maybe he was right.

Maybe I was becoming him.

Or worse –

Maybe I already was.

# 15

The aluminium coffin finally reopened on the fifth floor, and I fell out into a warm corridor.

There was nobody around as I looked both ways, but I was sobering up, so I hurried down past the doors, trying to find what I was after.

Val Vulva's room was 534. And after some walking back and forth, I found it.

A strong stench of cannabis had crept from underneath the door and this had helped in my search.

I stood in front of the door and listened. I had imagined the sound of partying, or at least voices – people arguing about syringes and how to correctly OD. Yet there was nothing. It may as well have led to a cemetery.

"What are you doing?" I whispered to myself as I tried to glance through the one-way peephole.

I didn't know what to do now.

*Should I knock?*

*Should I try to force my way inside?*

Suddenly sobriety kicked me up the arse and I realised how stupid I was being. This wasn't just investigating the claims of a jealous husband – this was breaking and entering, trespassing, intruding, obstructing intravenous drug use, or whatever.

"Go home, Hassle. You're drunk!" I told myself the same thing everyone else had been telling me since I was fifteen.

But just as I went to turn, I saw the door to room 534 creak open...

It was unlocked.

And this changed everything.

My inherent curiosity forced me on. The same curiosity that had made me the best P.I. Moseley had to offer. And the same inherent curiosity that my mother had had in rough men, which ultimately led to her demise.

I placed a hand onto the door and pushed it open.

The hotel suite was large inside. It was open plan. There was a lounge area with a large television, leather sofas and a glass table perfect for cocaine abuse. Off to one side, there was a shadowy kitchen that seemed untouched – but I knew that junkies never ate.

Still, the most striking feature about the room was its morbid silence.

(I had compared the silence to a cemetery. And little did I know just how much the two would have in common…)

"Val?" I called out into the room, but my echo was the only reply.

Quickly I moved inside. I closed the door behind myself and started nosing around.

What was I looking for?

I found some bottles of Amstell in the fridge, so I stole five of them. I necked one, opened another, and stuffed the other three down my jeans.

On the kitchen worktop was a record player and a pile of old vinyl.

I leafed through.

I found the first pressing of *Electric Warrior* by *T. Rex*.

I smiled and put it on.

Marc Bolan's soft voice began to fill the emptiness in the room.

In the lounge area I found neat lines of white powder, cut and waiting on the glass table. I was tempted to have one…

*What the hell! It's a Wednesday. Treat yourself, Hassle!*

However, I decided not to. There was no way of telling what it was – cocaine, heroin, bath salts, parmesan?

While staring at the white dust, I noticed lights flashing from behind me. I turned around and saw a bedroom door was open. It was dark inside, but the whitey-blue flashing of a muted television danced through the shadows every few seconds. Someone must have been in there…

"Val?" I called out again.

I considered shouting *Mr Vulva*, but I just couldn't bring myself to do it.

As I approached the bedroom door, I felt a strange feeling begin twisting about in my guts. Instincts were warning me. My footsteps slowed as I tried to listen to them:

*Something bad has happened in that room,* they said.

And they were right.

Lying dead on the bed, was Val Vulva.

I recognised him from the photo Stod had given me. His hair was still dyed blue, but the colour had faded since the picture was taken. Although it seemed impossible, he also looked even more emaciated and thin.

Blood, fresh not dry, had run from either side of his mouth and settled into puddles on the bedsheets.

Just another drug overdose, I thought to myself. But then I looked closer -

His eyes drew me in –

They were glazed and terrified –

He had not died well.

As I checked for a pulse, to confirm what I already knew, I found his neck was broken.

I lifted his lifeless carcass up and his head fell backwards, hanging off his shoulders and touching the middle of his back. His neck had been snapped completely in two.

"What the fuck happened to you?" I asked the corpse, willing it to answer and name its killer.

I gently lowered him back to the bed.

I had finished my second Amstell.

*Could he have fallen? Drunken or high?*

No way. That was impossible. He was lying on a soft bed, not the sort of surface that could do the damage he had. Plus, his injury would have killed him instantly – no time to crawl up and die on the mattress. No, no, no. Someone had murdered him. And *just before* I had arrived.

"What are you doing, Hassle?" I found a sensible sober thought ask me, just like it had before, outside the room. "You're getting pissed-up at a murder scene!"

(Even for me, that was a bit excessive.)

I left the bedroom and threw the bottle of beer away.

Then I looked out the window into the Birmingham night. It was glaring back in at me, returning my gaze.

*It* knew who had murdered Val Vulva. It had watched as he inhaled drugs up his nose and squirted them into his veins. And it had also watched later in the night when someone had snapped his little junkie neck in two.

As I stared transfixed into the night, feeling poetic, I almost didn't notice the flashing red and blue lights from the street below.

I peered down.

And my mouth ran dry...

Three panda cars –

Police cars, parked outside the Radison with doors open and empty seats.

I knew immediately what was going to happen -

The door to the hotel room swung open –

I caught a momentary glimpse of police uniforms.

With the speed of a cougar at dusk, I dove into the kitchen and prayed that they hadn't seen me.

Thanks to heroin's appetite suppression, the kitchen was untouched and cloaked in darkness.

I watched as four coppers rushed obliviously past me and into the bedroom.

*Thank god! You can always trust Birmingham's finest!*

I grinned to myself in the shadows.

*This is your chance! Get out, now!*

There could have been more police in the corridor.

I didn't know. But I had to try.

Quickly I rushed out of room 534.

The corridor was empty. So I continued walking quickly down to the lifts. When I got there, I smashed the button to send me down to the lobby so I could escape.

I watched as the numbers lit up, slowly rising from the ground floor.

My heart rate - up. My time - limited. My future - always in jeopardy.

From behind me I could hear footsteps.

*Shit!*

They sounded heavy and thunderous. I imagined some bulky, ginger-haired Irish plod, swinging his nightstick and itching to fuck someone up.

The footsteps grew louder and louder.

They were coming my way.

Sweat burnt my forehead.

*Don't let them take you alive, Hassle!*

I wiped my forehead.

*Fuck! Fuck! Fuck!*

I didn't have Putlog on me. God, I was a useless bastard! What was the point in having the fucking thing, if I never took it with me?

I had no choice. I would have to punch. I would have to punch with my fists. I balled my hand up into a vicious lump of flesh and fury.

*They will regret it! They will regret it!* I assured myself.

The footsteps stopped behind me.

And warm, corn-beef-smelling breath began lapping against the back of my neck, like some repugnant, post-war tide.

*NOW!*

In a spinning right-hook, the envy of even Steven Seagal, I felt someone's face fold over my fist. Then I heard them collapse to the ground.

I looked down -

It was an old white woman wearing a turban.

She must have been in her seventies.

"Bollocks," I said, just as the lift doors opened.

A hotel maid stepped out and paused at the scene in front of her.

She looked at the unconscious old woman, and then back at me. Then she screamed and dropped all the towels she was holding.

"There has been a terrible accident!" I said, moving her out of the way and getting into the lift. I hit the button for the ground floor. "She was complaining about her mind and then she fell. Oh god, oh god, oh god no, oh god..." I kept saying that until the lift doors shut. Then I sighed. *What a fucking nightmare!*

But before I had a chance to compose myself, the lift stopped on the fourth floor and two policemen stepped in.

The lift doors shut and both coppers stared at me, hard. They were studying me, reading me, trying to break me, trying to make me breakdown crying just with their stares. My bruising and swelling surely didn't help.

I tried to resist their pressure.

I was squirming inside my own skin, but I tried to resist.

Then one of the bottles of Amstell fell down my trouser leg.

It broke on my foot but was still hidden under the jeans.

Foam began pouring out from under the cuff, over my shoe and the lift floor.

"Who are you?" one of the coppers demanded.

*Think fast, Hassle!*

"I...am...Tuuurrbb...erm, Turrrb... Maaaaaid. Yes, Turb Maid."

(WHAT THE FUCK WAS THAT?)

"Who?" the other copper scoffed.

*Say it with confidence, Hassle!*

"Turb Maid!" I tried to speak confidently, but just sounded really aggressive.

The two policemen looked at each other, confused and maybe a bit freaked out.

"What is your business here?" the first one asked me.

"Well, I'm staying here, aren't I?"

"I don't know. That's why I'm asking!" he barked.

I said nothing.

"What is your business in Birmingham?" the other one asked.

"I... am... reading poetry."

*Oh Jesus...*

"You're a poet?" he asked.

"No."

They looked at each other again.

"I mean *yes, yes* of course. *No* is the title of one of my poems."

*A-ha! Good one, Hassle!*

"Let's hear a bit then," the first copper smiled evilly and nudged the other one. I couldn't tell if he was suspicious and trying to call my bluff, or just a bully who wanted to humiliate me.

*Fuck.*

"I never repeat my poems," I stuttered.

"But you said you were here for a poetry reading?" the other one said.

"Yes. I do so, in silence."

They said nothing, just seemed confused, so I tried to surround my excuse with bullshit:

"It's a political thing, man! We are all silenced by the patriarchy! Don't you get it, man?"

The first copper stood forward and pressed his helmet against my forehead.

"Let-me-hear-a-poem!" he grunted.

It was definitely the strangest sentence to say in a threatening manner.

I smelt cheap coffee on his breath, and it woke me up. There was no getting out of this. I would have to convince them and convince them well, or I could be leaving here in the back of their car.

"What is it about? This *No?*" the other copper asked.

"Rape," I said quickly.

It was the first word that came to mind. (Worrying... yes, I know.)

"Oh my," he gasped.

"Let-me-hear-the-rape-poem!" the first one grunted.

I stood back from him and cleared my throat. As I opened my mouth, I had no idea what was going to spill out, I just hoped it wouldn't get me arrested...

"NO!" I began. "You, you, should not rape.

"NO! Don't you see your ills?

"NO! Put your fascist phallic ph-philosophy far, far away!

"NO! No more, no...erm, no more shoplifting lesbians -,"

The first copper held his hand up. "Enough."

For the next few moments, we were in complete silence as the lift descended. Maybe they were amazed by my adlibbed poetry, or maybe they were disgusted.

When the lift finally opened on the ground floor, all three of us stepped out.

There was a plain-clothes detective talking to the receptionist. He was barking orders at her and she seemed stressed.

I noticed more police had arrived since I'd looked down from Val Vulva's window and they were milling around in the lobby, talking to people and causing a fuss.

"We need to secure the scene people!" I heard the detective start to shout as I passed him by.

"DID YOU HEAR THAT, EVERYONE?" the first copper from the lift shouted out loud. "SECURE THE SCENE! THE PERPETRATOR COULD STILL BE IN THE BUILDING!"

Just as the orders to lockdown the hotel began swinging into motion, I slid between the automatic doors unnoticed, out into the safety and danger of the Birmingham night.

I felt wild.

I felt crazy, lucky, stupid and alive.

I pulled an Amstell from my jeans and twisted the cap off between my teeth. I spat it into the gutter and sent the sweet release down my throat to drown the terror inside me.

My mind had opened a ricin letter.

Everything was racing a million miles a second.

What the fuck had just happened?

Was I involved in someone's murder?

# 16

I had been set up.

It took me half a pack of Chesterfields and the rest of the Amstell on a park bench to figure it out.

My train-of-thought had been fucked-up. I wasn't thinking right. So I'd took the 50 bus to Kings Heath and walked into Highbury Park. It was dark and lonesome, so I wandered over to a bench near a secluded pond, sat down, drank, and smoked, and pondered. It was a warm, purple night with a cool breeze running through the trees and grass. I liked it like that.

A gang of teens with a bull terrier had walked past me. They were spotty and scabrous, and the desire for trouble seemed to illuminate behind their cider-soaked eyes, but luckily for them I was in no mood. I had bigger worries –

Stod had set me up!

Greasy fucking Stod.

It was him who had given me Val Vulva's address –

He had sent me there –

He knew I would be there –

He knew where to send the filth –

It wouldn't have been hard to keep tabs on me. I was probably followed from my office or The Elizabeth, and then to the Radison hotel.

That seemed like the obvious answer, but I was still confused.

Maybe Stod did find out I was shagging his wife. But wasn't having me framed for murder a tad extreme?

And then there was the other blazing question –

Who killed Val Vulva? And why?

Did Stod kill him?

No way, he didn't have the bollocks, or the physicality to end a life.

Surely Val wasn't just killed to frame me?

There had to be more to it. And I had to figure it out.

This web of deceit I had flown myself into seemed to grow and grow. I felt wearier and wearier as the fag ends piled up by my feet, building into a cancerous mound.

My patience was wearing thin. I wanted to go home but I couldn't. Not tonight. My DNA was all over the murder scene - the door handles, the fridges, the beer, Val himself... Soon they would be knocking at my door.

I had to find Val Vulva's killer.

*And* clear my name.

*And* all before the coppers caught up with me.

Otherwise, I was fucked.

"No warm bed tonight, Hassle," I said to myself.

The gang of teens glanced briefly back at me, but they must have thought I was a dangerous lunatic because they carried on into the night.

Alone and cold, I swung my legs up onto the bench and curled up.

The stars above me were barely visible through the smog, but I looked at them anyway, and the freedom they offered. They were just like me, trapped in smog, a flicker of hope, trying to get out, yearning for freedom. That was what I thought about, as the wind between the trees and the grass sung me to sleep.

# 17

I awoke at the crack of dawn. Light danced majestically across the crystal surface of the pond water and skull-fucked me in the face. I was hungover. I didn't need light. I needed eternal dusk.

A man walked past me. He was in his fifties. He was holding a doggy bag that was full. But he had no dog. He was smiling. I waited and waited, but no dog followed. Had he filled the bag himself? Or had he taken it out of the bin to bring home? I didn't know. I wanted to ask, but I didn't.

That horrible creeping feeling of self-disgust accompanied the horizon. They were good friends.

"Is this it, goddamnit?" I spat at the day.

I felt entitled to more. No more nights in Highbury Park when I was lamming it. From the cops, from the dealers, from the clients, from...well, whoever.

*But what good did I do?*

Surely the world was give-and-take.

And I sure took more than I gave.

"Well, I..." I tried to think up the good deeds from my past.

About the only thing I could think of was pissing the skidmarks off the toilet pans in The Elizabeth. That was what I *gave back* to the community, and I never asked for any thanks either.

That was the limit of my morality.

Maybe that's all I was –

A morality skidmark.

I knew it was time to leave when a homeless man joined me. He started singing some Neil Diamond song and it scared me. I felt vulnerable. He kept getting the lyrics wrong and looking at me like I should appreciate the whole thing.

I got up from the bench.

"Good morning," he said.

"Yes."

I cricked my neck and last night, in full recollection, hit me like an uppercut on the inside.

"I have the bends," the homeless guy said.

*The bends?* I thought, looking at the pond. *Had he dived in and not exhaled on the way up?*

"Right, good luck with that."

Then I noticed both shoelaces of mine were undone.

Had this maniac-with-the-bends undone them during the night?

I was unsure.

It was time to leave.

I decided to go back to the office. I didn't know whether it was a good idea or not. But I was hungover and didn't care. A bed in Kings Heath police station suddenly didn't seem too bad.

Before I walked up the hill, back into Moseley and back to my office, I visited a twenty-four-hour outdoor in Kings Heath. They were always open and they sold everything - even the imported stuff that the nutters in the car parks and alleyways drank.

I got a pack of Chesterfields and a single tin of Holsten.

On the walk back up the Alcester Road, I cracked the can.

The froth was warm, but that didn't matter.

I sipped it.

I felt better.

After a few glugs my dreary headache withered and died and anxiety about being arrested for murder seemed ludicrous.

The hill also didn't seem that steep.

I would sort it.

No worries.

No worries at all.

*Because I was Paddy Hassle…*

*The best fuckin' P.I. in town!*

# 18

Jesus Christ, I felt like shit.

I waved at the blokes downstairs who were smiling at me on the way in. I went straight up to the office and changed. I swapped my dirty jeans for some less dirty jeans, took the leather jacket off, swapped the black t-shirt with the cigarette burns for the black t-shirt with the mustard stains, put the leather jacket back on, pissed, brushed my teeth, and took a long look in the bathroom mirror at the greatest sleuth born of his mother.

"You've got this, our kid!" I told him.

(But shit, he already knew.)

I loaded up the laptop. I needed to contact the band that Stod had mentioned, the one that Vulva was in. But I couldn't remember their fucking name. They might offer some clues that could aid me in clearing myself.

On Facebook, I saw my ban was up.

I opened it up and found the link to a poorly written article by Birmingham Live. It concerned the death of a local musician in the Radison hotel.

"Well, if you aren't my man, then that's one hell of a coincidence!" I chuckled and clicked on it. (The Holsten had gone to my head.)

The name of the victim was given as Andy Head, not Val Vulva, but I supposed that that was his stage name.

It said police were treating it as a murder investigation and wanted to speak to a man who had previously spoken to officers that night – in other words, *me*.

"The Gulldongs!" I said out loud when I spotted the band's name.

It gave a brief mention of Val Vulva's music career as an up-and-comer. The Gulldongs had played The Dark Horse, Sunflower Lounge, and supported at the O2 Institute etc. etc. It seemed they were well accepted but deemed a bit too heavy for the commercial world. Nevertheless, the critics predicted a bright future for The Gulldongs.

(The article also mentioned the assault of a seventy-five-year-old clairvoyant. Her name was Mystic Ann, and she had been set to perform that night at a local bar, reading palms and contacting the deceased. It said that someone had broken her jaw by the lifts and police believed the crimes were connected. Mystic Ann was in a stable condition in hospital. But she disputed the police claims, saying the perpetrator was in fact a disgruntled spectre.)

I found The Gulldongs fan page on Facebook. They had several thousand likes.

I messaged them, saying I needed to speak with them urgently.

While I waited, I went downstairs to the shop.

There was a man in the queue trying to buy bread and lager, he had no money but demanded he be allowed to have it. He claimed he was *The Lord of the Homeless*. I couldn't be bothered to listen to it, so I went outside and smoked a Chesterfield while I waited.

I needed to quit smoking.

A good P.I. should be able to sprint one-hundred yards in seconds.

I finished the fag and saw there were five left in the pack.

I gave them to The Lord of the Homeless, bought some Holsten and went back upstairs.

The Gulldongs had replied to my message with a phone number. There were some words along with it, but they made no sense. My intuition told me that the messenger was intoxicated. The only word spelt correctly was *fuck*.

I called the number, cracked a can and leant back in my chair.

"Yo," a rugged voice answered.

"Yeah, who's this?" I asked.

"Yo, who is this?"

"I'm asking the questions here, pal."

"You called me."

"Is this The Gulldongs?"

"Who wants to know?"

"Paddy Hassle, that's who. That name mean anything to you?"

"Hmmm…" the voice considered something and I heard bubbling, lots of bubbling, followed by exhaling, coughing and laughing. "*Hassle?*" the voice sounded choked, then returned to normal. "I think I've heard of you, man. You solve shit, right?"

"Fuckin' A."

"You want to come round, man?"

"Yes, to ask some preliminary questions."

"Oh shit! Sounds serious."

"It is. Where do you live?"

"The Red House, my man. The one that Jimi sang about…"

"Talk sense, you pot head!"

"Trafalgar Road, man. The Red House. You can't miss it…"

I heard more bubbling and then the phone went dead.

Fuck…

Hippies.

Hippie musicians…

This could get ugly.

Real ugly.

# 19

I started chewing Dulse.

It was seaweed from Ireland and it tasted like salt, only saltier.

The old man used to chew it to take the burn of liquor off his breath at work. It would substitute the smoking, I decided. My version of Kojak's lollipop.

The first handful tasted good. It mixed well with warm lager.

Alcohol and salt. I'm sure my digestive system would thank me.

*For Pete's Sake* was playing by *The Monkees* from the stereo.

I duct-taped Putlog to my forearm. This time I wouldn't be caught without him. If these rabid hippies tried to jump me, then they would pay for it.

I put the leather jacket over the top and inspected myself in the mirror.

"Listen you fuckers, you screwheads..." I attempted to begin the monologue but didn't have the energy.

I packed Dulse, finished the can, and split.

I walked down to the junction in Moseley. The lights were saying one thing and the cars were doing another. The streams of traffic were punctuated every so often by an entitled cyclist. I hated cyclists. From their lycra to their toned calf muscles, something about them just stunk of wankerdom.

Eventually I crossed the road to the square. This was the centre of Moseley – the square. There were benches, lampposts, and hedges, all surrounded by bus stops. People called it the square, but I called it the graveyard. It was the mecca for the local undead druggies and dribbling juiceheads. They swarmed the area, getting in the way, causing trouble and being a general nuisance. All the signs on the lampposts around them prohibited the drinking – but they didn't care - and the hundreds of panda cars that went up and down the Alcester Road every day, didn't care either.

I think these scumbags flocked to Moseley because the area was so *right on*. The leftist population accepted them, cuddled them, gave them vegan wraps and told them how brave they were. Anywhere else in Birmingham they would either be murdered or ate.

"Hass, Hass, my man!" someone shouted.

I turned and saw one of the undead approaching me.

It was the same guy from The Elizabeth the other day. The one who had smelt of B.O. and failure. I remembered that he had pissed me off, but I couldn't remember what about.

He was wearing a suit, but it was dirty and torn. He had a can of cider in his hand and was out of his mind.

I hated the fact that these kind of people knew my name.

"What do you want?" I asked.

"Got a cigarette?"

"I quit."

"Fuck you!"

"What did you say?"

"Please man."

"Look, have this," I fumbled in my pocket and handed him a fistful of Dulse.

"What the fuck is this shit?" he glared at it.

"It's Dulse."

"What?"

"I'm chewing Dulse instead of smoking now. Take it."

I turned to leave, but barely took two steps before I could hear dry heaving from behind me.

I turned around and saw the man bracing himself at the knees. His can of cider was rolling down the road. He kept retching but not vomiting anything up. One strand of drool lowered from his lip, lower and lower, touched the pavement, then he sucked it all back up.

"What have you done to him?" someone started screaming.

I looked up and saw a flock of menopausal women rushing over to him.

It was Moseley Market day. Shit. This happened on Saturdays. The population of Moseley came out to flog hemp, cucumbers, cotton, paintings, cheese, sculptures and other shite.

"I've done nothing," I protested.

"We saw you! You poisoned him, and just because he's homeless! You should be ashamed of yourself!"

"Listen," I pulled the packet of Dulse out. "I gave him Dulse."

"Well, what is that?" one of them snapped at me.

(She must have been the brave one.)

"Seaweed," I said.

They looked at each other. *"Seaweed?"*

The first one shook her head. "A new strain of cannabis, no doubt. These horrible dealers come down here and hand out free samples to the homeless population, try to get them hooked on it!"

(She must have been the gob-shite one.)

"How awful!" a third one sobbed, then actually started crying and had to be hugged by another.

(She must have been the depressant one.)

"You people are mental," I couldn't be arsed to argue with them, so I walked away.

He was still dry heaving, and they were patting him on the back.

Fuck, I needed a Chesterfield.

# 20

I bought forty Chesterfields from an off-license I hadn't used before and sparked up.

The cigarette tasted good.

Mrs Stod smoked the same brand, and the taste reminded me of her lips. But in turn, that reminded me of Stod, the set-up, the murder, and all the other bullshit... Suddenly the Chesterfield didn't taste so good.

I persevered with it though.

While I walked, I flexed Putlog under my arm. I smirked to myself. No one knew he was there. People may have underestimated ol' Paddy Hassle, but they had no idea the chaos he could cause.

I passed by a bloke in a leather jacket. The jacket was okay, but he had it zipped up. That was a problem.

Carrying on through Moseley centre, I took a right down Woodbridge Road. I passed by some more shops and paused outside of Patrick Kavanagh's – a local pub.

Foolishly, I decided to walk inside.

"Pint of Guinness," I asked the bartender and they got to pouring it.

Pat Kavs was okay, I suppose. It verged on the Kale and Corbyn of Moseley which I detested, but still had a large Blues (Birmingham City Football Club) element which, although I loathed all sports, kept the pub grounded and kept the bearded crusties away – to an extent.

I recognised a table in the corner where a gang of tradies used to drink and discuss timber, roof tiles, and concrete.

One of them was a painter. He was wearing flip flops and seemed drunker than the rest. I noticed he kicked his flip flops off to go to the toilet. That just seemed plain wrong.

The bartender asked for something close to a fiver. I handed him a tenner and walked to a table with my pint of plain and a fistful of coins. Life didn't seem too bad.

Guinness relieved my thirst (probably instigated by the Dulse).

I sat and relaxed, coming up with a game plan –

How would I approach these Gulldongs?

And what information did I need to get from them?

I needed to find out if they had a relationship with Stod. Did Val Vulva have any enemies? I needed to get closer to exposing the true killer, and if I could prove Stod's involvement in my framing then that would be the icing on the cake.

"Ha-ha-ha!" I laughed to myself, sipping Guinness and imagining Stod being molested in a Winson Green shower.

The painter returned from the toilet, still bare-footed. He looked at me while I laughed to myself, frowned and continued back to the table.

A smile was on my face.

Was it the Guinness? The image of Stod being buggered to death? Or was I just *feeling good?*

I felt in the mood for music.

I put a few pieces of shrapnel into the jukebox and hit the sixties tunes -

*Connection* by *The Rolling Stones*

*Boom Boom* by *The Animals*

And *Straight Shooter* by *The Mamas and The Papas* (a personal favourite and very underrated tune. In fact, an underrated band in general.)

The Guinness went down well. It must have, because I had two more and needed to take a slash.

I left a half-pint settling on my table and walked into the back, to where the toilets were.

In the gents, I unzipped at the urinal and took care of business.

Behind me, in the locked cubical, I could hear someone snorting. They were snorting really loud. At first, I thought they were doing it to cover up the sound of them taking a crap, then I supposed it was just really enthusiastic drug abuse.

While I was still pissing, the cubical door opened.

A man stepped out.

He didn't look right.

He looked like Uncle Fester from the Adams family, but after some tragedy that he wasn't handling well.

"Alright, haaaaaa, mate? Haaaaa," he kept panting like he'd just finished a run. "Haaaaaa."

"Yes, I'm fine," I said, trying to hurry up and finish so I could get out of there.

"You enjoying yourself? Haaaaaa."

"Erm, yeah," I tensed all my pissing muscles, trying to speed it up.

"Good, haaaaa. Are you, erm... Haaaaaa. Okay though?"

*Fuck sake!* I tried to stop pissing, but as any man knows, it isn't easy. I put myself away and felt mini spirts of urine go down the inside of my leg. I was angry.

"Yes. I'm fine. What the fuck do you want?"

"HAAAAAAAAAAA," he started panting louder, maybe nervous.

I left the toilet.

*The Mamas and The Papas* were just ending when I sat back down.

I lifted the last half-pint of Guinness and sipped at it quickly.

The Uncle Fester guy was stood in the veneer of the men's toilet door. He was sticking his thumb up at me.

I finished the Guinness.

Trafalgar Road, where The Gulldongs allegedly lived, was just past Pat Kavs.

I left the pub and glanced up at the painting they had of *the* Patrick Kavanagh who had originally opened the pub. It sickened me. The egotism. The notion. *What kind of man names a pub after himself?* I thought. The Gareth Arms? And why was this *Patrick Kavanagh* so important, more than any other landlord. Why were other old pubs not named after their owners? That would be far better, real pubs, in psycho areas, with paintings of their original owners - toothless, mental Victorians with syphilis, not some prick in a beret with circular glasses.

(Circular glasses! Another thing to mind. Men with small hands is number one. But men who purchase circular glasses is another. They all must think they're Trotsky, and I would happily do the pic-axing for them!)

"Enough, Hassle!" I said aloud and the painter glanced at me again.

Misanthropic melancholy was marauding through my mind.

It distracted me at times, I needed to keep focused.

I walked out of Pat Kavs and took a sharp left down Trafalgar Road. I passed by some cars and kept my eyes out for a red house.

Would it be obvious? I asked myself.

A cat ran out from nowhere and startled me.

I was feeling a tad pensive, and I didn't know why.

Then I heard it...

Guitar, bluesy guitar and a familiar voice...

*"There's a red house, over yonder*

*That's where my baby stays..."*

It was the song.

It was *Red House* by *Jimi Hendrix.*

Was I imagining it?

I followed after the music. The guitar and vocals grew and grew. I was becoming excited. Giddy even. Giddy on Guinness and stoned on Hendrix.

Then I saw it –

An old Victorian house, painted scarlet red.

The upstairs windows had bedsheets over them, but light illuminated from within. The one window was open, allowing music to sail down while the sheets stirred in the wind.

I could smell smoke, hear laughter and saw silhouettes of figures shuffling from within.

The Gulldongs awaited.

# 21

I knocked the door and waited. Nothing. I heard the voices from the upstairs window and considered shouting up but didn't.

Instead, I called the number again.

I told the voice that answered that Paddy Hassle was outside and, if they valued their front teeth, they better put down the pot and open the front door.

Thirty seconds or so later, it creaked open...

A lanky looking bloke with long hair, five-day stubble and baggy t-shirt was Clint Eastwood-ing at me. He wasn't trying to intimidate. He just hadn't seen sunlight for a day or two.

"You pot heads are like vampires," I said, gently moving him back inside and following in after.

(I never liked cannabis, marijuana, grass, whatever. I had no doubt for some people it induced bliss. But personally, it made me feel like a potato - un-peeled - in a kitchen draw - doing nothing - wasting my time and waiting for the roots to sprout. I never spoke sense on it. I never thought good. All I did was smile like a simpleton. No, not for me.)

I followed the guy up a set of stairs and through an open door. He told me on the way up that the house was empty. The top floor flat, which The Gulldongs rented, was the only occupied one.

We went into a living room.

Jimi had finished. They were listening to *Mona* by *Quicksilver Messenger Service*. (Must have been a 60's psychedelia playlist.)

Another guy was in there. He looked like the smaller Russian doll version of the first. He was wearing a poncho. He smiled as I walked in, but I had the feeling he was smiling when the room was empty just the same.

"How you doing, dude? I'm Hopper," the small, poncho guy held out a hand.

I shook it.

Formality.

It was clammy.

I made a mental note to wash mine.

"And you?" I gestured to the first guy, who was leaning up the wall and still Clint Eastwood-ing at me. "Micky Sphincter?"

Hopper laughed.

"No, bro. Why'd you think that?"

"Well… vulva, sphincter, arsehole. I suspected it was a trend. Why did he call himself that anyway? Absolutely disgusting."

"Oh man," the nameless guy swatted the air and sat down by Hopper. "You couldn't tell Val what to do about nothin'."

I sensed a genuine sadness from the pair of them when I brought Val Vulva up. I admired that. They were true friends.

I sat down and lit a Chesterfield.

"Hey man, can you smoke outside?" the nameless one asked.

"Are you joking?"

"Yeah!"

He and Hopper started giggling together.

I took the notepad and the Berol out of my jacket pocket. I slid the Chesterfield across to the corner of my mouth, so questioning could begin.

"So – you, wiseguy, what's your name?"

"Patrice."

I made a note, although I thought it was probably bullshit.

As I finished writing, Patrice, the chatty one, started again –

"Hey man, are you really Paddy Hassle?"

I looked up. *A fan?* "Yeah, what of it?"

"Is it true you caught the Howard Road Strangler?"

"Damn right."

Hopper spoke up. "Shit, I remember that! The dude that kept strangling himself in front of people with a belt. That shit was freaky."

"Yeah, well I got the bastard."

"Cool, man. Real cool!" Patrice started nodding like one of those Bulldog toys. It started fucking with my flow.

"Can you stop nodding?"

"Yeah, sure man. Sure."

But he kept on nodding.

"How'd you catch him?" Hopper asked, he seemed like the smarter of the pair.

"Not that it's any of your business... But I hung around the local belt shops. Looked into the forums online that those perverts use. Then patrolled Howard Road, religiously."

"Oh, you prayed?" Patrice asked.

*"What?* No."

"You said religion."

"Forget it, Patrice."

"But you got him though?"

I nodded. "Indeed."

These two chatty pot heads were messing with my flow, and I forgot what questions I was planning on asking.

"Hey man, is it true you caught the Hound of Highbury Park?" Patrice asked again.

"YES!"

"Holy shit..." Hopper hit a spliff. "I remember that, man. People kept getting mauled by it."

"Yes. It wasn't a dog at all, it was a man dressed as one. He used to operate in Hall Green, then relocated," I explained.

"No waaaay!"

"No shitttt!"

"Freeeeaky, man."

"F-reeeeeaky!"

They both burst into laughter.

It gave me time to collect myself and prepare the questions.

"What are your full names?"

Hopper held up his hand. "Billy Sanderson, but like I said, they call me Hopper."

I made note.

Patrice held his hand up. "Patrick O'Neil. But like I said, people call me Patrice."

I paused. *"Patrice?"*

"Yeah, man."

"So that's... *Patrice O'Neil?"*

"Yeah, man. What's the joke?"

I shook my head and moved on.

Just as I opened my mouth to ask a follow-up question, the door opened by itself. My muscles instinctively tensed up and I was ready to jump up and slam an aluminium-clad-forearm into the intruder.

Patrice and Hopper must have seen some kind of madness in my face, because they immediately shouted –

"Hey, chill, Hassle! It's only Scratch Man!"

The door opened further, and the Uncle Fester guy from Pat Kavs stumbled inside. He was sucking his lips and wide-eyed. He started to smile until he spotted me and then he started panting again.

"Scratch Man, this is Hassle," Patrice motioned.

Scratch Man tried to say something – ended up panting – and I grunted a *hello*.

"Did Val's mom like the flowers, Scratch?" Hopper asked.

Scratch Man looked at me. "Yeah...yeah she did..."

Patrice smiled and started nodding. "Good, man. Good. Did you hear that, Hassle? We all chipped in for flowers for Val's mom. Isn't that good, man?"

I smiled. "Oh, how lovely." Knowing that the *flowers* had been sucked-up Uncle Fester's nose about a half hour earlier in the pub. "They must have smelt beautiful, now sit down, will you?" I'd had enough of looking at him.

Scratch Man walked over and sat by the rest of them. He said nothing, just shifted an intense stare between whoever was talking. (But he remained quiet, which was the main thing.)

"Now, do either of you -,"

"Hey, Hassle, check this out!" Patrice pressed the TV remote and music started blaring -

It made me jump -

I turned and looked -

It was a music video of, I could only assume, The Gulldongs.

They seemed out-of-control by a canal. Jumping around with their instruments while the thrash-metal blared all around them.

"Turn that off!" I shouted, but they couldn't hear me.

"TURN THAT OFF!"

Patrice turned it down.

"Jesus Christ, I'm trying to ask questions!" I snapped.

"Sorry, Hassle. I just wanted your opinion."

I looked at the TV. "It's, it's okay..."

"You like it?"

I paused again. "What genre is it? Punk...thrash...grunge..."

Hopper spoke up. "Nah dude, it's Meth-rock."

The other two agreed.

"Can we carry on with the fucking questions now?"

They nodded and politely waited to be asked.

"Do any of you know a man who goes by the name John Stod?"

For the first time since I'd arrived - silence.

They looked at one another.

Hopper spoke first. "Yeah, man. He's our manager."

Stod - music producer. The Gulldongs - band.

*How had you not put this together already, Hassle?*

I jotted some things down.

"Has he been managing you long?" I asked.

Patrice and Scratch Man started messing about with something, I wasn't paying attention. Hopper however, was decent enough to talk.

"Not long. About a year or so."

"How do you get on with Stod?"

"Stod's an asshole."

"So you do know him," I laughed.

"No, man. He's a serious asshole."

"I know."

"Man, I'm serious. He ripped us off big time."

"How so?"

"Well, he wined and dined us a few times, got us high, got us laid, took us to some wild parties, got us playing some cool gigs. Then he got Val all fucked-up on H and convinced him to sign a contract on behalf of all of us. Dude, it's a joke. Let me think... We are unable to record any other music with any other band, or solo, until the contract is relinquished... The contract is for nine-hundred years, by the way... We cannot earn money through any other music recording, as producer, session musician or whatever... And if any money is made from our material – which he owns all of by the way – we get two per-cent royalties, minus any *unforeseen expenses*. Stod is an asshole man, a fascist, a Kristallnacht asshole."

I was impressed at the way he recounted it.

And I admired his Kristallnacht reference.

Patrice suddenly butted in. "Yeah, but it's not all bad, man. He's selling our contract to some other dude."

Hopper sighed. "I suppose, he might be cooler."

"Who's he selling you to?" I asked.

"Don't know, man," Hopper answered. "He treats us like mushrooms dude, feeds us shit and keeps us in the dark."

I had a clear link here, between John Stod and The Gulldongs.

I didn't, however, have motive for Vulva's murder, nor the identity of the actual killer.

Stod was playing games, and I wanted to flip the board and thumb the bastard in the eye.

"What about you two, you're awful quiet," I nodded at Patrice and Scratch Man.

"What's to say, man?" Patrice answered while Scratch Man panted.

"About Stod," I asked.

"He's naff. He's a spaz. 'Nuff said.'"

Suddenly Scratch Man grabbed a guitar and started playing it.

"Did Stod get on with Val?" I asked.

Patrice sniggered. "No way. Stod and Val are from two different universes, galaxies even!"

Scratch Man was still strumming the out of tune guitar.

"Put that banjo down!" I shouted and he did. "Back to Stod and Vulva, why didn't they get on?"

"Like Patrice said, man. They were chalk and cheese," Hopper started. "Stod wanted us in the studio twenty-four-seven. He wanted us sober, recording, practising, doing the corny interviews he set up for us. All to line his fucking pockets! And Val just wasn't about that."

"No way!" Patrice shouted. "Val was living *the life*, man! He had it made!" (I remembered finding his corpse... yeah, some life.) "Women, drugs. Val knew how to live life, bro. You can never take that away from him."

I smirked. "Well someone did."

Gloom descended on the room, and I noticed Patrice and Scratch Man had been cutting up lines of white powder.

They must have noticed me looking, because Patrice spoke –

"It's the only way we can cope, dude..."

He lowered his head and snorted.

Then he passed the DVD box with the white lines across to Scratch Man.

"Haaaaaaa... yeah," Scratch Man rather cleverly said, before doing his line.

Hopper did his and then they all looked at me -

There was a fourth line left on the DVD case -

Hopper held it out to me in one hand -

And a rolled-up tenner in the other -

"You want?" Hopper asked.

*Pablo Picasso* by *The Modern Lovers* was beginning to play from whatever mishmash playlist they had on in the background.

*I should have an early night - my first of the week...*

I needed rest, to keep myself sharp, alert and thinking straight, but, well, but -

I accepted the tenner half-heartedly.

And then the DVD case.

"Ah well, fuck it," I said and they all giggled. I put the Berol pen away. "Enough work for one day, I suppose." They laughed again. *"When in Rome!"*

Patrice grabbed my wrist. "No, dude... *When on Trafalgar Road.*"

# 22

Fat white slugs slithered across the table, into a note, up our noses, and down the back of our throats.

The slugs filled your body with confidence, your mouth with bullshit and your brain with fantasy. I had been there before. But that didn't stop the devil's dandruff from taking over. That's what I didn't like about it. But hey, it was only the one night, I supposed.

We listened to music and shared stories. Everyone jittered. The floor jittered. People struggled to keep their mouths closed. No one listened. Only waited to talk. No one watched. Only waited to be seen.

Cocaine was an awful drug, I decided. An awful high and an awful deal. For the money and the hangover. It made you socialise with people you never would do sober, talk about topics that don't interest you and plan activities you have no intention of doing in the future. With cocaine there is only *now*. You can't help but talk about eternity, but eternity ends when the baggy does.

"You ever seen us live, Hassle?" Patrice asked me.

"No, I haven't."

"Well, dude, I've got your number now. I'll let you know when we're next playing.

"Okay."

"It would be sweet if you came."

"All right, I will."

"Remember our last gig with Val?" Hopper chimed in.

Patrice and Scratch Man started laughing, laughing to cover up the sadness. They felt pride in their deceased rakehell of a comrade.

"What happened?" I asked.

"It was a shit gig. Stod reckoned we needed to tone down our image and appeal to a more universal, PG kind of audience. So he booked us to play in this park. We didn't know it, but it was a Bible reading. Can you believe it?"

I couldn't help but laugh. Then I hit a tin of some cheap lager they were drinking.

"An all-female Christian rock band were headlining - *The Birds of Pray*. We just had to support. They were like Karens in their forties - short hair, fat arses, glasses, and those red cheek things."

"Yeah, man!" Patrice exploded. "The main chick had that vein shit going on in her chin. Vas-a-vasca-,"

"Viscerous veins?" I asked.

"Yeah, man."

"On her chin?"

"Yeah, man. You should have seen that shit! It looked like the Atlas in there. I could see the A435 connecting to the Stratford Road, dude."

We all laughed.

"Hey, man! Let me finish!" Hopper said. "So Val had found out about this, and somehow found the time to spare his partying cash and buy a priest fancy dress outfit! He performed the whole show in that shit, and you know something? Those Bible bashing nutters didn't say a word. They were in awe. They actually thought he was a priest. We went down a storm. We could have sold a single to every fucker in that audience."

"Yeah, cudda…" Scratch Man added.

"Yeah, until the afterparty."

"What happened?" the sleuth in me asked.

"Well, Val had lost his shoes. He'd taken some horse tranquilisers at the end of the show. So he walked in there…"

As Hopper continued on, I thought for a moment –

Val Vulva hadn't deserved to die.

I mean, I didn't know the full story at this point. But the kid was just a musician. Yeah, a bit of a drip with the drugs, but he seemed like a laugh, like a genuine wild soul. And I knew, somehow, that he had been killed for selfish reasons. Probably for money. Maybe to frame me? Maybe just for that. Maybe I was the reason he died. But either way, at that moment, high on cocaine, in a shit hole flat with his best friends, I pledged to do the dead kid justice. I would find his killer...I would make them pay, and I would bring them to justice.

# 23

Time goes fast on uppers. The night seemed to end and sunshine rise before I'd had time to take a piss.

Suddenly the sun was burning through the bedsheets they had over the windows. The beers were drunk. The powder was sniffed. The TV was muted, and everyone looked at each other in a certain disdain. Regret at what they'd said and done, and a longing to reclaim that *connection* the narcotics had brought between them, and then taken away. Suddenly, and silently, the drug abandoned all of us and left us as strangers in a room together.

The Gulldongs started rolling joints. They would get merrily stoned to avoid the hangover, maybe nap and then start all over again.

"Fuck that!" I said, making them all jump.

I stood up and stretched.

I thought booze could make me feel like death – but this was something else!

"You going, Hassle?" Patrice yawned, Scratch Man was asleep on his shoulder.

"Yeah, I'm going."

"Okay, dude. Well nice meeting you."

"Okay."

"I'll let you know if I hear anything."

"Right."

I never mentioned that I found Val Vulva, or that I was the one the police were after. That would have been foolish. I needed to play these naive, friendly rockers. It was immoral. But that was who I was, and that was what I did – I played people.

I walked myself out the flat, down the stairs, and out of the Red House into a blistering sun on Trafalgar Road. This was not the kind of morning that I needed.

I had memories of being stood in a twenty-four-hour petrol station with Hopper on the Brighton Road, arguing with the owner about the price of Stella. That was only a few hours ago but felt like another lifetime.

And then other memories of performing one of Sickle Cell Anaemia's classics for The Gulldongs to hear. They'd liked it. "Really?" I'd gurned at them, with the guitar over my thigh.

All in all, during the course of the night, I'd actually *joined* The Gulldongs, started a solo project with Patrice and agreed to help direct a short film about graffiti artists in Digbeth.

"What the fuck!" I said out loud, scaring a cat – the same cat that had startled me the day before. "Fuck cocaine."

I needed rest.

# 24

My grandfather always told me: *never poach eggs in the nip.*

I then understood why.

I was bollock-naked in the flat, watching the egg whites turn opaque in the bubbling water. I was starving. I hadn't ate since... well... I couldn't remember. I'd found a couple of eggs in the fridge and decided to do the right thing. But my clothes seemed greasy and stunk of cigarette and ganja smoke, so I threw them off while I waited for the water to reach the boil.

The top decks of the 50 and the 35 could see me, though I guessed most passengers doubted their eyeballs. *Surely no man cooks eggs naked?* They must have said to themselves... as I did.

I scalded myself several times and decided the long-dead mick was right. I should have at least worn undergarments.

When I showered, the comedown eased. I turned the water up and tolerated it. I hated showering hungover or drunk, it usually made me feel ill, but this time it didn't.

I had a Holsten with the poached eggs and felt like Hassle again.

Energy started thundering through me - from the hops in the Pilsner and the protein in the yolks. I felt invincible. I felt like the greatest bastard ever to grace the earth. This was it! I decided. No drugs, no nothing. Just natural alcohol, good old-fashioned alcohol. And ingested naturally - not sniffing it up your fucking nose, shoving it up your arse or kneeling in it. This was substance abuse the old-fashioned way. And it worked.

I listened to *Frankie Valli & The Four Seasons* while I relaxed.

They were singing *Dawn (Go Away)* and it was what I needed at that moment in time.

"Now time for business," I said, dropping the dishes in the sink and taking a seat at the office desk. "Stod..."

I needed to pay that little shitheel a visit. A balaclava visit. There were too many unanswered questions that he could resolve for me, maybe after a bit of finger breaking.

I could waste the rest of my life creeping, sleuthing, and scheming to get the answers I needed.

*Who killed Val? Why? And why was I framed?*

But I decided to cut out the middleman and go to the source!

Not only that, but I was running out of time. I could feel it. The filth would be here soon. That would be all I needed, stuck in a cell, no solicitor, and no chance against a bloke with the money and connections of John Stod. I needed to clear my name and find those responsible before the long arm of the law caught up with me.

"In fact!" I burst out, taking my naked feet off the desk and starting to pack a bag.

I was being foolish. I needed to keep out of the office, or at least take measures to lam it if they showed up.

(The boys were singing *Ragdoll* now.)

My road-kit included: a change of clothes, toiletries, laptop, phone, a couple of CDs, Putlog, a bag of Dulse and the final few tins of Holsten that had been chilling in the fridge.

Then I called The Gulldongs:

"Yo," Patrice answered.

"Patrice. Hassle."

"Hey, man! How's the head?"

"Not good. I need to talk business."

"Pop round, dude. We've got a line with your name on it. Oh, and we've got E's! Proper nineties E's! Not the new MDMA powder shit. This is proper! Come round! Come get Ian Browny with us, bro!"

"Put Hopper on."

"You still rehearsing with us tomorrow?"

"Errr... Just put Hopper on, will you?"

There was a little kafuffle on the line -

"Hey, Hass," Hopper said.

"Hopper, have you got Stod's home address?"

"Yeah, sure. Gimmie a sec…"

More kafuffle -

"Hass, you still there?"

"U-huh."

He gave me an address on Reddings Road and I hung up.

"Son of a bitch…" I grinned, smiling at what I had just written down.

Reddings Road was a two-minute walk from the flat.

Stod was a Moseley-ite.

Perfect.

I finished getting ready. Lit a Chesterfield. Pulled on the leather. And wore a flat-cap low on my brow. This required some covert measures to be taken, I decided.

*The Aquatones* were singing *You*. (It was my Doo Wop playlist.)

Downstairs, I told the lads in the shop about my little *disagreement* with the local authorities and they knew exactly what I meant. They agreed to give me a signal when I returned later, to let me know if the filth had arrived.

I also left the flat light on and curtains open upstairs. If the coppers accessed my flat and wanted to lie in wait, they'd turn the light off to remain discrete.

Across the street, I hid the road-kit in a hedge behind the bus stop by the local post office. Hopefully I wouldn't need it, but better safe than sorry.

"Now time for that shitheel…" I lit another Chesterfield.

# 25

It was a sunny day in Moseley. Nice, even. The Holsten I'd removed from my road-kit was ice cold and it went down nicely.

Carrying on up the hill, a couple passed me by. They were professional types, pushing a newborn in a pram. They looked too old to have a kid, but people were doing that more – waiting until the last minute to have one. Through fear of death. Fear of dying alone with no hand to hold. They must have been late forties, the bloke maybe even fifty. *He'd be good fun down the park...* I thought to myself. When the kid would be twelve, the dad would be sixty-two? Shattering his pelvis trying to catch a frisbee.

They had glared at my can of lager –

Why? –

Drinking in public –

Still a taboo.

*But where is the line?* I asked myself.

If I was a bird with nice pins in Highbury Park, drinking a fruit cider and listening to Radio 1 – then that'd be okay?

Vice versa – the human excrement on Moseley square, necking super and shouting at Staffordshire bull terriers, then that wouldn't be?

"It's all madness!" I cursed the world.

So where did that leave me?

Where did that leave a hardworking son-of-a-gun like Hassle? Minding his own business and taking a few hits of Holsten.

The world didn't make sense to me. But I suppose it didn't have to.

I walked past Moseley hospital.

There was a bloke waiting for the bus. He was wearing a leather jacket, but the jacket was too long. It was down by his shins. Long leather jackets make you look like you have Asperger's.

The last house before the turning onto Redding's Road had a black

Ford parked on the drive. It was dirty.

I was looking at the car when the front door to the house opened –

A girl came running out. She had a lot of life in her eyes and a smile on her face. She was wearing a beanie and had bombastic coloured trousers. She was drinking one of those pre-mixed-cocktail-tins. I tipped my hat to her as she passed by, and she giggled a *hello*.

"Still got it, Hassle," I said to myself as I turned down Reddings Road.

A hundred yards or so down Reddings Road, I found Stod's house.

It was a palace of a place, with a wall and waist-high gate to keep the proletariat out.

He also had a Daimler on the drive.

*What a prick*, I thought. *Who'd he think he was? Some paedophilic monarch?*

For a while I just smoked Chesterfields and walked slowly back-and-forth, past the house and on different sides of the road. I wanted to come up with a plan.

It was a quiet afternoon, a lazy afternoon. Most people were relaxing watching television or pottering around their gardens. It was perfect for me.

After I built up the courage and got a vague idea in mind, I hopped the waist-high gate and strolled casually past the Daimler, down to the house. (There was no CCTV I could see.)

The side-gate was locked, but it was easy enough to pull myself up and over.

I landed gently on the other side and paused again...

The side-entry led down to the garden. Halfway down was a door to what looked like the garage or utility.

I walked down to it and tried the handle –

It was open.

Inside, I walked through the utility room. Past shelves of cleaning products, a washing machine that was running, some tools and other shit.

The door at the end led into the kitchen.

It was a modern kitchen, a big open-plan thing that also involved a dining and sitting area. The whole place, however, was empty and silent. If I didn't know better, I'd say the house was deserted.

Butterflies were in my stomach.

I lived for this.

I was giddy and excited, moving around the kitchen.

I stole a handful of cherry tomatoes from the fridge. (Just because I could.)

In the kitchen window, I watched someone in the garden hanging up washing at the far end. It was a breezy day, warm too, perfect for drying.

The woman wasn't Mrs Stod, no way. Her hair was too short and her legs were too fat. She must have been a cleaner or a maid or something.

The ground floor was deserted. I found a lounge and separate snug area. No sign of Stod and no sign of an office – which is what I was really looking for.

I'd have to go upstairs...

The mahogany staircase creaked on each tread, as I tried to scale them stealthily.

At the top I found a landing area with door after door after door – wide open, with neat, untouched beds, drawn curtains and pristine carpet. It didn't look like Stod had any kids, at least not in this house.

At the far end of the landing, were two more doors. One was shut and the other was open. Through the open door I found what I was after – his office.

Stod wasn't in it, but his laptop was on and his desk was cluttered with papers and business documents. I started snapping pictures of them on my phone for evidence. I was panicking to begin with, taking pictures of anything, then I started to calm down and approach it more sensibly.

The first thing I determined was that financially, Stod was in trouble –

Bills... bills... bills... court summons... CCJs... maxed out credit cards... sheriffs notices... repossessions... accounts in arrears...

"So much for a big shot," I mumbled to myself.

The man was desperate.

The Daimler was set to be repossessed. The mortgage was behind on his Redding Road palace and his music production company was near bankruptcy.

Murder suddenly didn't seem so out of the question.

Not for a money-hungry, desperate little runt like Stod.

I documented it all, then I started on his laptop.

I searched through his *Recent Files* and found one called *Gulldong Sale Draft*. I opened it up -

It detailed the sale of The Gulldongs contract from his ownership to another individual. The same shitty, blood-constricting predicament that Stod had had The Gulldongs in, was simply being passed onto someone else.

"Poor guys. They don't stand a chance..."

The names of the band members were listed:

William Anderson. (Hopper)

Patrick O'Neil. (Patrice)

Jack Fraser. (Scratch Man)

But there was no mention of Val Vulva. Not one mention in the whole contract. I remembered that Val Vulva's real name was Andy Head, but there was no mention of him either.

I checked the whole of Stod's computer through a search - and found not one mention of him.

"What the hell's going on?" I asked myself.

But a search of the computer's recycle bin led to multiple files about Val. Stod had deleted them. Stod was erasing him from his computer, erasing their relationship, erasing Val Vulva's very existence!

"Check the date of the new contract," I told myself.

I went back onto the *Gulldong Sale Draft* and checked the date of its creation...

Bingo!

The file had been created *before* Val Vulva's death.

Stod had drawn up a contract to sell The Gulldongs, not including Val Vulva, before his murder.

In other words, Stod knew he was going to be killed and drew up the contract without him.

This was the kind of evidence I needed.

This proved Stod knew about Val Vulva's impending death, but it didn't explain motive.

Sale of The Gulldongs - well sure - to help settle his accounts.

But why did Val Vulva have to die?

Nevertheless, I took pictures of it all and forwarded myself the relevant documents through email. Then I deleted the internet history of me doing so, thus covering my tracks should Stod check.

The last thing that stuck in my mind was the name of the buyer – the individual who would be the new manager of The Gulldongs:

Theo Oak.

"Who the fuck is Theo Oak?" I whispered to myself.

I had no idea. I'd never heard of him before. But worst-case scenario, this Theo Oak was another lead. Maybe he was involved in the murder too? And maybe he was the weak link I needed?

Time to split, I decided.

I turned to leave the office, but saw the door across the hallway begin to open...

# 26

It was the dame - Mrs Stod.

"How're you doing?" I asked before she saw me.

She nearly shrieked in horror, so I jumped forward and clamped a hand over her mouth.

"Paddy!" she struggled with me. "What are you doing here?"

I pushed her back into the bedroom and shut the door behind us.

The bedsheets were all a mess. She must have just got up. On the bedside table there were a few prescription medicines and an empty bottle of wine. She'd been washing down Valium with Jacob's Creek pinot. Not a bad afternoon.

"Take it easy," I said and took my hand off her mouth.

"Jesus, you're insane, you truly are insane!" she turned around and sat back down on the bed. Her eyes were glazed. The pills had hold of her, or the grapes.

"Like I've got a choice? Your hubby has framed me for murder!"

"What?"

"Yeah, no bullshit."

"I warned you about him, didn't I?"

"Listen -,"

"Didn't I warn you? But *ooooh noooo*, big man Paddy Hassle doesn't worry. He just swaggers around like John-fucking-Wayne, doing whatever he wants, to anyone he wants -,"

I put my hand back over her mouth. She was inebriated.

"Keep it down!"

"I don't have to keep it down in my own house!" she wrestled with me.

I pinned her down on the bed. "Don't push me, baby!" I clenched a fist.

She laughed and wrestled free. But she did, however, calm down.

"You need to leave, Paddy."

"Where is he?" I asked.

"John's out. John's always out."

"He's in trouble."

She said nothing.

"Well, I know he is." I continued. "And whether you like it or not, looks like you'll be back on the streets."

Mrs Stod got back into bed, under the sheets. "No way. John wouldn't do that to me..." Her eyes started to shut.

"Hey! Wake up!" I shook her.

"What? What?"

"Wha-d'you mean - *what?* I've got to clear my fucking name! I'm on the lam. The murder squad are after me! You need to help me!"

"I can't help you, Paddy."

"Why the hell not?"

"I'm not getting involved."

I paused for a second. The bitch was making my blood boil. "*Not involved?* Why you precious, little slut. It's your fucking fault! If I'd never -,"

She sat up and smirked. "*If you'd never...* what?"

I said nothing.

"Exactly," she scoffed and fell back into the pillows.

I sat down at the bottom of the bed, by her feet.

"It's all to do with this band. This fucking band The Gulldongs. I just can't make it all add up!"

There was a moment of silence and then she spoke. "Paddy, you really have to go, for both our sakes."

She was right.

But I couldn't let this opportunity pass me by.

She must have been able to offer some information that could help.

"Who is Theo Oak?" I asked.

I watched the glaze leave her eyes.

The name woke her up.

"He's - he's just an associate of John's."

"Don't dick with me, baby."

"He does a lot of different things. He runs those professional wrestling shows in the city... He has some casinos in Chinatown... Some clubs... He puts raves on... This and that, you know?" she was spieling off horseshit.

"What do he and Stod have to do with each other?"

"Paddy, I've said enough. I'm not saying anymore."

"This Theo Oak - there's something you're not telling me!"

"He's bad news! I don't know what he's really into. Drugs - maybe? But he's a big shot. He's got a lot of men working for him, okay?"

I pondered it for a moment.

Maybe I was onto something here with Oak.

*Gangster?* Could he, or one of his buttonmen, have been the one who *pushed the button* on Val Vulva?

Mrs Stod was looking at me intensely.

She looked good.

"You want me, don't you?" I asked.

"I want you to fuck off, if that's what you mean?"

I smiled, and she did too.

Then I stood up.

I thought about Stod. I thought about how much I hated him. What he'd done to me. This palace he lived in. The woman he shared it with. The car he drove. The money he had. The way he ripped off The Gulldongs. The way he framed me for murder. And most of all - what he'd done to Val Vulva.

So I threw my flat-cap away and kicked my boots off -

It was only right, I did this –

I jumped onto the bed -

I had a duty!

"Paddy, what the hell are you doing?" Mrs Stod started laughing, a crazy laugh, an inebriated, hellfire and brimstone, no-shits-given, prescription-abuse kind of pinot grigio laugh.

"Fuck you, John Stod!" I shouted.

I didn't care if the cleaner heard.

# 27

The sky looked like skin filling with blood by the time I left. Dark bruises of clouds across a sheet of purple velvet. It felt eerie. Gloom seemed to drift down like invisible rain. I didn't feel safe, and I wasn't exactly sure why.

I upturned my collars and pulled the flat-cap even lower than it was normally. My hair was sprouting out the sides, thick auburn curls. I needed a haircut. I needed to find a real job, a real home, and a real life.

"Sometime," I said, sparking a Chesterfield and strolling down through the dark evening, back down Reddings Road, to the Alcester Road and to where I could head home.

I could never make it work with a woman like Mrs Stod. I understood that. And almost absurdly easily, any feelings I once had for the woman seemed to eradicate themselves within me. *Was I cold-blooded? Or something else?*

"No time," I muttered through a gob-full of cigarette smoke.

No time for existential ponderings. I was a murder suspect. First and foremost. I needed to clear my name.

I needed to find Theo Oak.

And I had a feeling that my good pal Apollo Somerfield would know him, or of him. He could offer me something in the way of help.

By the time I reached the shop, and my flat above, I almost didn't notice the lights had been turned off upstairs.

*This is it...* I realised.

I had been biding my time, running on a sheet of thin ice, above dark, deep, freezing waters. And now it had cracked -

The law had found me.

And almost on cue, one of the lads downstairs stepped outside of the shop with a cigarette.

He saw me –

We met eyes –

He nodded –

I understood –

The number 50 was pulling up –

I grabbed the road-kit from the hedge by the post office –

I jumped on –

Paid –

Didn't look back –

Didn't hesitate –

The murder squad –

PCSOs –

Every plod on the beat –

Pig in his panda car –

Would have my picture soon –

The manhunt would be on –

I needed to hurry –

I needed to hide –

And I knew where to go –

Where I would be welcomed –

Where people *like me* went to hide away.

## 28

The Rowton Hotel (not to be confused with the *Radison*, where I found Val Vulva) was a place of squalor in Digbeth, Birmingham town-centre, ten minutes from Moseley.

It was built just after the turn of the century, as a boarding house of sorts. It would take anyone; tramps, drunks, criminals – those who couldn't convince private landlords to let them a room.

The Rowton asked no questions. It had a shady history. Crime was rife, and many lives ended within their tiny rooms...

Delirious alcoholics swallowed their own tongues, suffocated on their own vomit, or succumbed organ failure after lifetimes of misery and inebriation. The mentally ill, the insane, the drug addicted and the drug-sick, strangled themselves to death, overdosed, drowned in the bathtubs, or opened their veins to end their suffering.

Prostitutes used it to service their customers. Criminals used it to shelter their dealings. And others used it simply as a place to hide.

During its time, it also operated as a half-way house for nonces and sex-cases, out of prisons or facilities and unable to find a place to live.

The vulnerable occupants of the Rowton suffered theft, assault, and rape – mostly unsolved, very few even reported.

All these transients called the Rowton their home.

And now I was going to join them...

On the number 50 from Moseley into Digbeth, I'd gone upstairs and hidden at the back of the bus.

Unfortunately, at the next stop a madman joined me.

He was drinking a can of beer, was obviously drunk, and dressed entirely in high-vis clothing.

"I work the cranes in town," he kept saying.

"Okay, great."

"They've kicked me off site."

"Oh no."

"Failed a drug test."

"You're kidding."

"Nah, mate. They reckon I tested positive for opioids."

"Oh dear."

"It's bullshit. I told them: I eat bread with poppy seeds on. That's what done it."

"Well obviously."

"They don't understand. They don't know fuck all."

"Yeah."

I couldn't take much more, so I hopped off a stop or two early and walked the final bit to the Rowton.

Digbeth was dark and raining, and I didn't feel like dawdling.

I walked quickly. I kept my bag held tight. And my eyes sharp to every shadow, every alley and every possible hiding place. I'd been mugged once a few days ago, and I didn't fancy it happening again.

When I reached the Rowton, I was soaking.

I walked straight inside and up to the reception. The lobby was old-school art deco. It looked like the hotel from The Shining, and I suddenly felt the urge to kill a black chef with an axe.

"Room for one," I asked the receptionist.

She nodded and handed me a key.

I found the lifts by myself, headed up, found the room, let myself in and locked the door behind me.

I was exhausted.

The room was tiny and quiet - morbid and dead.

It was like a coffin for the not-yet-dead, but the not-truly-alive.

"It'll do," I silenced the criticisms in my head.

I went to the bathroom and found an unflushed piss still eroding away in the toilet. I flushed it down and shivered.

Using my beard-trimmer, I shaved my head, altering my identity.

I cleaned up, put the hair in the toilet and decided not to flush.

Then I went to bed in the darkness.

Outside the window I could hear the wind.

I liked hearing the wind as I slept.

It reminded me that I wasn't dead yet.

There was still a world out there.

And there was still life left within me.

I had time...

# 29

The next morning, I hit a fistful of Dulse and took to the streets. I needed to clear my mind and start thinking straight. This had knocked me off my axis – having to lam it again. I was wobbly. And not only that, but the old man was nearby again. I could smell his breath behind doors, beneath floorboards and outside of windows. I needed to keep cool.

(*Take a moment. Take a moment to remember you're Paddy fuckin' Hassle, the best goddamn P.I. Birmingham has ever seen!* I told myself.)

The swelling on my face had nearly vanished now, but I assumed it was part of the description the coppers were looking for.

So I put on some foundation. (Yes, laugh it up...)

With the foundation on my cheeks and faded blue bruises like eyeshadow, I must have looked like the King of Hurst Street (or maybe the Queen?).

But I didn't give a shit.

I'd hit a can in the room and taped Putlog under my jacket.

I was ready.

Digbeth could throw its worst at me.

*And oh boy, it sure did...*

I saw her and recognised her immediately, but it was too late to turn around. She had spotted me, and pride kept me walking forwards.

"Patrick Hassle, why your mother must be turning in her grave..."

"Good morning to you too, Mrs O'Toole."

Mary O'Toole was stood outside St Anne's church. Her brow-beaten husband, whose name I couldn't remember due to irrelevance, and with eyebrows that needed trimming, just held his shabby suit up and stared at the pavement. I figured that was all he was good for.

"And what are you doing with yourself nowadays? Still philandering into other people's business? Still drinking yourself stupid?"

I couldn't be bothered to reply.

When I was a kid, Mary O'Toole was an old bag.  And now that I was grown-up, Mary O'Toole was still an old bag. It didn't make sense.

"And where are you living?"

"The Rowton," I pointed, then felt stupid for letting it slip.

"By god!" she raised a hand to her mouth. "Just like your father."

"What are you talking about?"

"When she first met him, your dear mother, that was the hell-hole he called his home."

"Nonsense."

"No, it-is-not-nonsense! She used to bring his meals and nurse him back from his binges. And I could never understand it. How that lovely, young girl would bother with such an animal like him. All those trips, all those nights walking up to room two-oh-two."

I had done talking with her.

"Goodbye, Mrs O'Toole."

"Goodbye yourself!"

I turned the corner from St Anne's just as the rest of the congregation spilt out onto the streets.

I checked my pocket for the key to my room -

I checked the number...

"Fucking hell," I grunted.

The smell of whiskey-breath was strong suddenly.

I wandered around aimlessly and found myself outside of a pub called the Town Crier. It looked like a fucking dump. But I was pissed-off and didn't care. So, I walked inside anyway.

Immediately the landlady started giving it large:

"TAKE OFF THAT JACKET!"

"What?" I asked, genuinely confused.

"TAKE IT OFF! THAT JACKET!"

"Fuck," I took off the jacket and didn't understand why. I folded it around Putlog, so he remained unseen.

The pub was empty except for the accommodating landlady and a lone-drinker with a boss-eye. He looked like he was staring at me, or maybe the door, or maybe fuck knows.

I walked over to the bar.

"Well what do you want?" she snapped.

"Erm, just a beer."

She sighed and handed me a can of Carling. I didn't ask why it was a can, not a glass (I assumed a problem with glassings). And I didn't bother asking for something else, seeing as I detested Carling, which I thought tasted like watered-down blood.

"Where do you live?" she asked.

"Why?"

"WHERE DO YOU LIVE?"

The can of watered-down blood didn't seem worth this abuse.

"The fucking Rowton."

She glared at me. "Are you Irish?"

"Yeah."

"What kind of Irishman rents a flat?"

I paid and then she walked off.

I was confused and insulted.

I sat down and opened the can.

The boss-eyed cunt was staring at me (I think) and I was getting closer and closer to the edge. His head was covered in scars and so too were his knuckles, it looked like he was so-so in his fighting skills.

"Lot of strangers in here tonight..." he said (meaning me).

"It's ten in the morning."

"Yep, lots of strangers..." he sipped his can.

He seemed like the kind of loon who started on his own shadow for standing too close.

And I assumed he probably said the same thing on Christmas mornings in his living room.

I decided not to get into trouble.

I sipped the can and texted my Uzbekistani friend.

I needed my new wheels.

I couldn't rely on walking or public transport, it left me too vulnerable.

After ten minutes or so, he got back in touch and agreed to drop it off at the Rowton for me.

I finished the can and put it down on the bar.

"Thank you for a pleasant morning," I said to the landlady and walked back onto the street.

Whether I liked it or not, I had to go back to Moseley. But I had to do so carefully. Covert. Undercover.

I needed to talk to Apollo and get some word on Theo Oak.

I was in a tough spot. The filth were after me and my flat was no longer safe. I did however have evidence that Stod was planning, or at least aware that Val Vulva was going to be harmed. I needed motive. I needed to find out why he had to die. And I needed to find the real killer. I needed a confession. And I was more than ready to beat it out of someone if I had to.

# 30

When I got back to the Rowton, he was already there.

He gave me the keys with a smile.

"And that weed in the boot. That was nothing to do with me."

I didn't say a word. I'd forgotten about that.

*How did that fit in with everything else?*

Stod?

No, he wanted me to take the fall for Val Vulva, not for some bloody weed.

Man, being Paddy Hassle wasn't an easy gig.

"Someone is playing you, my man," he said as he climbed into another car with a friend and disappeared up Bradford Street.

He was right. (He was ex-Soviet and deranged.) But he was right.

I clambered into the car and put on a CD I had been carrying in my leather jacket pocket.

*The Evil One* by *Roky Erickson & The Aliens.*

(Roky was a personal hero of mine. We had a connection. I won't bother going in depth. He was not of this world. Listen to this album and you can tell. The songs about zombies, vampires, fire demons, white faces, creatures with atom brains etc. all appealed to me. But I was OCD when it came to Roky, and when I started playing the album, I had to let it play all the way through.)

*Two Headed Dog* was the first track.

It was a powerful one.

A contender for one of his best.

I did a three-pointer and started back to Moseley. It felt peculiar. Moseley was my home, but I felt like an outlaw heading back to bandit country, somewhere I wasn't safe anymore, somewhere I had been exiled from.

"SHIT!"

The car in front of me did an emergency stop.

My heart fell in my mouth.

An elderly man got out of his car and started waving his fist at me.

"Turn that down!" he shouted.

Then he got back in his car and carried on.

*Was he on about the music?*

What had just happened baffled me.

I followed him up to the Mosque island -

We were in the same lanes –

He was going the same way –

He went over the island and into Basall Heath –

Roky was still screaming –

*"TWO HEADED DAAAAAAWG! TWO HEADED DAWG!*

*I'VE BEEN WORKIN' IN THE CREMLIN WITH A TWO HEADED DAWG!"*

Looking through his rear window to the front, I could see he had the wipers running at full speed even though it wasn't raining. They were on that setting that you never really used. If rain was that heavy, you'd have to pull over or die. But he didn't. Maybe he welcomed oblivion, as he tootled his way through Basall Heath, praying for a suicidal monsoon.

He stopped the car again and waved his fist again.

"Turn-it-blummin'-down!"

I turned it down a bit.

We got to by the Lidl and he stopped a third time, gridlocking the whole of the Alcester Road.

"Lower! Lower!" he shouted to me.

I lowered it. It was almost silent.

He got back into his car and eventually turned left up Trafalgar Road and nearly hit a woman who was crossing.

I passed by the petrol station, The Prince and the square. I could see the shop and my flat above it, but banged a left before it, heading up to Marks & Spencers.

I decided not to park too close, so I headed down Oxford Road and found a spot with no double-yellows or restrictions to leave the marvellous beige Juara.

In the rear-view mirror, I didn't recognise myself -

Not with a shaved head, low cap, foundation, and reddened sleep-deprived eyes.

I climbed out of the car, threw in some Dulse, lit a Chesterfield (yeah, I was doing both now) and started walking down to The Elizabeth.

It was a boring day, probably for most people. But not for me. Today could have been my last day of freedom. It felt like every action, every word, every thought I had, had to be done to prolong my liberty. I was, in fact, like a civil rights leader, an icon. I was like Gandhi, or Martin Luther King, or Pol Pot.

"Excuse me, mate. Have you got any -,"

"Fuck off!" I pushed some tramp away.

*What was I saying?* -

Oh yeah -

I was like Gandhi, or, yeah, whatever...

I reached The Elizabeth and prepared myself. I was sober and nervous. This was the most dangerous situation I'd ever gotten myself into and at that moment - I felt like a jerrycan of petrol hurling towards a bonfire.

Suddenly some slobbering pillock tried to talk to me, and that was all it took to force me through the doors and into the pub...

*To hell with it!*

## 31

The Elizabeth was the same as ever. It was no bullshit. That's what I liked about the pub. You left your subculture and your haircut at the door – or most likely it would get torn off.

Luckily, I remained unnoticed, slipping between two drunks and past an old woman who was singing and dancing by the fruitie. She was dressed overly provocatively, considering all her loose skin. She looked like an underdone roast chicken.

"It's great in here, isn't it?" I heard one eejit say to another.

"Aye, plenty of plant," the other eejit said, I think in reference to the old woman by the fruitie.

(I got sick in my mouth a little bit.)

Apollo was sweeping up a broken glass at the far end of the pub.

*Fucking typical!* I thought. If I'd wanted to avoid him, he would have been cleaning the glass on the front door.

"This world! This world!" I shook a fist to myself, low-key, remaining sleuthful, but never missing an opportunity to damn creation.

"Apollo, *pssssssssssstttt!*" I said as I got nearer.

He looked up at me.

And he recognised me in an instant.

"Oh Hassle! Oh Hassle!" he dropped the broom.

I was confused.

He grabbed me by both shoulders.

He didn't know his own strength and started to crush me into a smaller, narrower-shouldered man.

"HEY!" I yelped.

"Hassle, is it true?"

I wrestled free. "Is what true? What's wrong with you?"

"The diagnosis, man."

"What diagnosis?"

He buried his head in one hand. "The cancer!"

Oh Jesus Christ. "I don't have cancer, you fool!"

"But your hair man!"

"It's...it's..."

"Everyone in Moseley is talking about it, bro. *Hassle's lost his hair. Hassle must finally be dying.*"

"I don't have cancer, all right? And what do you mean: *finally dying?*"

He smiled, a big toothy grin. "Really? You're really okay?"

"Yes, well, yes, I'm okay. But what do you mean: *finally dying?*"

"Oh, forget it man!" Apollo swatted the air and hugged me, throwing me up in the air like a little kid.

(So much for keeping it low key...)

"Put me down, you big oaf!" I cried.

People were clapping and cheering, although I didn't think they knew exactly what they were clapping or cheering about.

"Apollo, I need to talk to you in private."

He nodded and motioned across to the cellar door.

We descended...

In the cellar, quiet and secure, he passed me a bottle of Holsten and started rolling himself a spliff.

"What's up then, brother?" he asked.

"I'm in the shit," I told him.

He nodded. "I heard the Babylon were sniffing round your place. What's occurring?"

"They're trying to finger me for a killing."

"Bloodclot!"

"Yes, that. One body. A musician, a junkie kid in town, strangled and had his neck broken in the Radison hotel. Only I'm innocent!"

"Bloodclot!" he licked the Rizzla.

"This bastard, this little bastard John Stod has set me up. Somehow, he found out I was shagging his missus. I never knew the girl had a fella, but anyway, he found out and has tried to pin this murder on me. The kid, the kid who died was called Val Vulva, real name Andy Head. He was in a band called The Gulldongs, I've met them – all right kids, nuts, but okay. Anyway, Stod was their manager. So he and Vulva knew each other, and supposedly, they didn't get along. Anyway, so I broke into Stod's house yesterday and I've got proof that he knew Val Vulva was going to get bumped-off. What I need now is to find the real killer and get the true motive. Some DNA evidence and a confession wouldn't be too bad either, you know?"

Apollo sparked his joint and pondered for a moment...

"So...you didn't kill the kid?"

I hit the beer. "No! Shit, Apollo. Keep up, will you?"

He puffed. "Sorry, man. Sorry."

"John Stod can't be the real killer. No way. But John Stod *is* selling The Gulldong contract to another bloke, and he's supposed to be a bit of a face in the underworld – a villain."

"Who that?"

"Theo Oak."

I watched Apollo's face closely as I said the name. My interrogation skills verged on the Schutzstaffel level. There was something there. He recognised something and suppressed something. Fear? Shock? Surprise?

"What?" I asked.

"Nothing, man," he shook his head, as smoke billowed all around him.

"You know something."

He started nodding. "I've heard the name..."

"And?"

Apollo reached over to the door leading back up to the pub. He pulled a bolt across and turned a key below.

*What was he doing?*

"You can't go back up there," he said to me.

"Why?"

"This man - this Oak… If I'm right, then you're in danger."

"Get to fuck."

"No, man. Hassle, this is serious."

"Is he capable of murder?"

Apollo tutted. "Like me and you boil a kettle, this man erases bredrin."

I didn't understand what that meant. But it sounded bad.

Then there was silence. As loud and lavish as he was, Apollo was a deep thinker, a descendant of Plato and Burning Spear.

"You scared?" I asked.

"I'm not scared!" he snarled at me like a Rottweiler. "But I'm scared for you."

I smiled. "I need to find him. Can you do your research, put your ear to the ground, find the word on the street?"

"Leave it with me."

"Right, open up," I pointed at the door.

"Go out the back," Apollo gestured to the back exit from the cellar.

"Why?"

"If this Theo Oak is who I'm thinking of, then he has friends all over the city. Friends…muscle…but most importantly a lot of nobodies who want to do him a favour. Nobodies who drink in Moseley too, and would be itching for an opportunity like this."

I understood. Any piece of shit, tenner-bag dealer could have spotted me walking in The Elizabeth. If they wanted brownie points from a face like Oak, then they could knife me as soon as look at me. Apollo was right.

We spoke for a minute or so longer.

We agreed to meet at The Fighting Cocks, a pub just up the road from The Elizabeth, before The Prince and near to the square.

We would meet the following night and I would use an alias.

I chose the name *John Butler Train*.

"I'll be seeing you then," I said, putting down my empty bottle and heading to the back door.

"Pad!" Apollo shouted after me.

"Yeah?"

"A lot of people were upset for you, man."

(He was talking about the cancer diagnosis.)

"Bullshit," I said.

"No bullshit. You've got more friends than you know."

That pissed me off. I took a few steps back towards him. "They weren't *upset*, Apollo. They just had another topic of conversation. That's all we are. And that's all our deaths will ever be one day... a topic of fucking conversation."

I turned to leave again.

"I think they cared," he said.

"Well, we'll never know," I said, carrying on to the door. "We'll never get to know who really cared, not one of us. You know why?" I opened the door and glanced back at him. "Because you can't go to your own funeral."

# 32

I was pissed-off again. I think it was those fakers in Moseley, using my non-existent illness as an opportunity to appear moralistic and more ethical than their co-wankers. They didn't care. They just wanted to appear like they cared. Death and illness were the perfect opportunities. They always came out of the woodwork when something bad happened. But god forbid you succeeded at something. Where were they then, to celebrate with you? Nowhere. They were at home, festering, green and jealous, praying for a cancer or an illness so they could cry and hug you, but giggle over your shoulder. I was adamant there was no such thing as a *good* deed – only deeds that made yourself feel good.

"People are a plague!" I decided, walking into an offie and buying a four-pack of Holsten.

I went back to the Juara, hopped inside, cracked a can and headed back to the nonce-hotel that I was calling my home.

*I Think Of Demons* was next on Roky's album.

I had been thinking of them too, until the devil's nectar crept down into my belly and sedated all my ills. That along with The Evil One's pained yet beautiful voice, made me feel okay.

## 33

I parked the Juara outside the Rowton and headed inside. The Holsten had gone to my head on the drive back and I must have been staggering about, because some old woman in a night gown started yowling at me in the lobby:

"Good god! That man is drunk!"

I ignored her and carried on towards the lifts.

"Mr Bundy! Oh, Mr Bundy!" I heard the receptionist calling after me, using the fake name I had rented a room with.

*Jesus Christ! Leave me alone!* I wanted to scream.

On the lift ride up, I decided I'd have to quit the Dulse. The receptionist told me there had been several complaints of a strong smell of salt coming from my room. I refused to divulge any information but assured her it would cease.

It was then that I realised I would have to do something I hated –

Wait.

Wait for Apollo to put out the feelers...and wait until the following night, when I was rendezvousing with him at The Fighting Cocks.

*I Walked With A Zombie* was playing from my battered stereo while I sat down.

I checked my phone.

The Gulldongs had called and I'd missed it.

I rang back -

"Hello?" one of them answered, it sounded like Hopper.

"It's Hassle. What did you call me for?"

"Oh, how's it going Hassle. I -," Hopper stopped.

There was a scuffle on the other end of the line. Raised voices. Struggling. The sound of a poncho being manhandled, and I could smell the marijuana cigarettes from the other end of the call.

"HASS! HASS!"

It was Patrice.

"What do you damn pot heads want? I'm a busy man!"

"Dude, we've got a gig. You said you wanted to come right?"

I sighed.

"Hassle, are you there, man?"

"I am here, yes I am."

"You've got to come, dude. It's going to be amazing."

"And why's that?"

"Our new gaffer has organised it."

My ears picked up, like a Doberman that had caught the whiff of an invading tramp. I smelt an *in*.

"Continue..." I said, resisting the urge to stuff seaweed into my mouth but instead lighting a cigarette (the guests didn't mind the smell of tobacco, it seemed).

"We met him today, man. He's a classy motherfucker."

"What do you mean?"

"He's like Jimmy Cagney, bro. Pin-striped suit, Brylcreemed hair, perfectly manicured moustache. Honestly Hassle, I was impressed."

"The gig! The gig!" I prodded.

"Oh, right. Yeah, so this cat – Theo Oak – our new manager, he has friends on the railways right. So once a year, this dude puts on this like insane party on a train. It happens at midnight, after all the services have terminated. He somehow gets his hands on a train, right? Then he kits the thing out, different carriages with different music, DJs, chicks, drugs, music, it's got everything, dude! And guess what, homeboy? The Gulldongs are playing the 'live band carriage.'"

This was perfect. I smiled to myself, dragging on the Chesterfield.

The Gulldongs could get me a ticket and then I was in. I had access to Oak and an opportunity to get closer to the real killer and some more hard evidence.

"Yeah, I'll go."

"What, really?"

124

"Yes. What do you mean?"

Patrice sighed. "Oh, nothing, man. I just lost a bet."

"What bet?"

"Hopper said you'd come. I said you wouldn't."

"So?"

"So... it means I'm seriously staring at sobriety for the next few hours, which isn't good, dude! I've got to split. I'll message you the deets, all right?"

Then the line went dead.

I lay down on the bed and finished the cigarette, staring at the water marks and peeling paint on the ceiling. I wondered how many other nobodies had lay on the bed staring at the same peeling paint, maybe smoking a cigarette, maybe not.

My phone buzzed and Hopper, not Patrice, had texted me a time and place for this party train –

*Wythall Train Station.*

*Saturday at midnight.*

I could meet with Apollo on Friday, then prepare myself for the party train and my shot at Oak the following night.

Things were coming together.

And in the rotting hotel room, I began to feel quietly confident.

Afterall, I was Paddy Hassle.

The best fuckin' P.I. in town.

# 34

I did nothing for the next day. My mind needed a time out. So I just lay on top of my bed and chain-smoked. I listened to music with my eyes closed, I lost myself in the darkness and kept imagining when I reopened my eyes that I would be somewhere else, somewhere better. But no, every time, still in the Rowton, still in Birmingham, and outside it was still fucking raining.

That evening the temperature dropped. A heavy frost descended on Digbeth and the surrounding areas. It seemed suitable for what was going on in my life.

Then I found myself on the number 50 bus, murderously pissed-off due to an unforeseen issue with the Juara.

I sat on the bottom deck. The seat beside me was empty. But I made a conscious effort to make steely eye-contact with anyone who got onto the bus, putting them off sitting next to me.

I found if you held their stare before they decided where to sit - they wouldn't sit next to you. If you were on your phone, or daydreaming looking out the window, it was less awkward for them to plonk themselves down beside you. The art of anti-sociability was one I was proficient in.

I got off the bus at Co-op and started the short ramble up to The Fighting Cocks.

The Fighting Cocks, similar to The Prince, was a landmark in Moseley. An old pub with a chequered history, it had functioned as a bordello and a music venue over the years. In the eighties it was punch-up central, but had mellowed recently. I liked it, the tiles on the walls and the stained glass in the windows were both older than the United States of America, and I found that amusing - *Greatest country on earth?* Don't make me laugh. *We have windows older than you!*

The Fighting Cocks was all right. In fact, I *liked* Moseley's pubs. The only problem with Moseley's pubs, was that they allowed the people of Moseley into them...

I had to be surrounded by vegan, feminist men with oestrogen levels so high in their body, that while I stood at the urinal to piss, they were in the cubicle – no, not partaking in healthy drug abuse – but changing their sanitary towels, either because they'd actually started having periods and synchronised with their other beta-male friends, or because their arses were that battered from the frequent poundings that their grizzly genderless girlfriends gave them, in an effort to erase the patriarchal sins of their forefathers one pegging at a time.

I shuddered.

I was talking myself out of going into the pub.

But I went in anyway.

I walked up to the bar.

"Hello," a young man said to me.

"I am John Butler Train," I told him.

He stared at me blankly. Then he looked frightened. He walked off and was replaced by another man. This guy was in his late twenties. He was thickly built, wearing a tight t-shirt but also a beanie hat.

*Why would you wear a woolly hat with a t-shirt?*

"Hello," the thickly built man said to me.

"Hello, do you have brain cancer?" I asked.

"Excuse me?"

Covering up a surgical scar seemed the only logical reason to wear a beanie with a t-shirt.

"Guinness, please," I said, and he eventually nodded and started on it.

I took my pint of plain over to a table in the shadows. The lighting was low in The Cocks, which helped me out.

In the corner I lay in wait for Apollo's arrival.

# 35

Apollo was an hour late, but I'd expected that. I'd sunk two pints of the black stuff and listened to Morrissey's cover of *Back on the Chain Gang* on repeat. It was a good cover, I'd thought. Yes.

Apollo had brought one of his ladies with him. A black woman with short hair and long legs. She was a stunner. The kind of woman you'd kill a cat for.

"Evening," I said when they approached my table.

"Evening, Hass," Apollo said.

"Shut up, you sleeze!" I said and pulled him down into a seat. "It's *John Butler Train...*"

"Oh, right, yeah..."

His lady sat down beside him.

"And who are you, doll?" I asked her.

"Ronda."

"Ronda, hello," I nodded, then went back to the black stuff.

"Apollo, babe, why are we sitting here?" Ronda asked. "They're all over there."

The stunner Ronda extended a long ebony arm and pointed to a table of champagne socialists. The men had beards but didn't deserve them, and the women needed beards but didn't have them. They looked like the kind of people who thought weightlifting was sexist. I was anxious at the sight.

"Oh, right, yeah..." Apollo sipped at a rum and coke. "John Butler, would you care to join us?" He stood up.

"No, actually, I wouldn't."

I tried to motion to Apollo, trying to say:

*I don't want to sit with those cunts.*

*What the fuck are you doing?*

*We were supposed to be exchanging information!*

"Oh, come on, John Butler," Ronda said and placed a hand on my shoulder. "We would enjoy your company."

I considered. "Well...okay then, Ronda."

I stood up, collected the Guinness, glared at Apollo and joined the champagne socialists at the other table.

(My fears were well founded.)

"Did you drive here, John Butler?" Apollo asked me.

"No, I fucking didn't."

The people at the table looked at me awkwardly.

"Something up with your car?" Apollo carried on.

"Couldn't drive. Some bollocks siphoned it."

"Oh dear, they siphoned the petrol?" one man at the table asked.

"No, the antifreeze, the screenwash."

"I don't understand," he chuckled.

"It's got alcohol in. The homeless have been stealing people's antifreeze from their cars around Digbeth to drink it. At least that's what I've heard. The windscreen was frozen solid and I couldn't defrost it in time. I got a bus."

"It's such a shame," a woman to his left said.

"Tell me about it. Six quid at the Texaco!"

"No, no. The poor man who took it. That he was that desperate, that dependant on intoxicants. Oh my, oh my..."

They all nodded in agreement with her.

They pitied the man who had robbed me -

Not the man who had been robbed -

Typical.

"Well anyway," another man at the table started. "I don't think they sell any *anti-freeze* in here!"

The table roared with laughter.

*What the fuck?*

That wasn't even a joke.

It was just an obvious observation.

Like saying –

Rape is bad.

Then everyone laughing at your fact.

I was running out of patience.

"Are we drinking or not?" Apollo spoke the first words of sense.

"Yes, yes!" one of the women grinned. "More sake everyone?"

"Oh yes."

"Please."

"It's vegan you know."

"And fair-trade."

"Awesome!"

"Great!"

*Sake?* The pretentiousness was vomit-inducing. Don't get me wrong, I *would* drink sake, if I was dining with Yakuza in Kyoto, Japan. But not when sat at a table of tossers in The Fighting Cocks. I added a Guinness to the order and it seemed to make everyone awkward for some reason, like Guinness contained the blood of a puffin or something.

When the Guinness and the sakes arrived, one of the glasses tipped over and spilt.

"Oh, for goodness *sake!*" one of them said.

The table roared with laughter.

I took my Guinness and left.

In the corner I listened to *She Bathed Herself in a Bath of Bleach* by *Manic Street Preachers*, all the while glaring at Apollo, summoning him over with my eyes.

Eventually he bit.

"What are you doing to me, Apollo?" I asked and signalled to the table.

He shrugged and sat down beside me.

"Spill it," I said.

"Tread softly, my brother, but carry a big stick."

"Oh, I do," I chuckled and patted Putlog underneath the leather.

"Dealing with Oak, you need to be careful. Brute force just won't cut it."

"I've got access tomorrow. The Gulldongs, the band I told you about, they're playing some gig on a train that Oak is hosting. He'll be there."

Apollo nearly choked on his sake. *"The Midnight Special? You're invited?"*

"What are you on about?"

"The Midnight Special. It's legendary across Brum!"

"A train... a party train or something, that's what they told me."

"Brother, you're in for a wild time. The Midnight Special! Shit, I thought it was just a rumour. Word is, the train will pick you up at a rural station, somewhere in the sticks."

"Wythall."

"That's it! It'll be loaded with rich kids, drug dealers and escorts. It should be wild."

"I'm not there for recreation, Apollo. I'm there to find Oak."

"And when you find him?"

I considered. "Well, I haven't figured that out yet."

"Paddy!"

"Look here, I think better on my toes, spur of the moment. I don't plan fuck all."

Apollo sniggered. "Your new friend Oak got *into it* last night supposedly."

"Oh yeah?"

"Yeah, bro. Just up the road at Sabai Sabai."

"Who?"

"The Thai joint by Pat Kavs."

"Oh...yeah."

"Some disgruntled former business partner spotted him and thought he'd make a scene – turns out *he* ended up being the scene."

"What happened?"

"He dropped a piece of soiled toilet paper into Oak's noodles."

"What did Oak do?"

"He perforated his mandibular."

"Fucking what?"

"Put a fork up through his chin - into his mouth."

"That's got to sting."

"Police came, took the man away, all the while Oak just re-ordered his meal, drank champagne and smoked his Marlboros inside. No-one-said-a-word."

"So, he's got clout?"

"He's got more clout than a trout with a pout."

"What?"

"Sorry brother, this sake is leaving me dizzy."

I laughed.

Then I noticed the Guinness was almost done -

So I stopped laughing.

"Serious talk though, Pad. You need a game plan. You need to be smart. You walk onto The Midnight Special with just your dick in your hands, you might never be seen again."

"Relax," I said and signalled the bartender for another pint of the black stuff. "I've got a plan coming together..."

"Well, good luck, man," Apollo stood up.

"Where are you going?"

"I'm doing a set."

"A what?"

"An acoustic session outside."

I watched Apollo walk away, out the back door into the beer

garden. I saw some sandal-wearing people walking to-and-fro with mic stands and string instruments. I wouldn't be joining them.

"May I sit down with you, John Butler?"

I turned and saw Ronda, Apollo's woman, standing beside the table.

"Certainly."

She sat down. She had finished her sake and was drinking a small glass of red wine. She had class.

"I've seen you around before," she said. "But I didn't recall your name as being John Butler."

"Well, now you know," I joked.

"You are friends with Apollo?"

"He's about the only friend I've got left."

Ronda sipped her wine. "Do you have a lady?"

I thought about Mrs Stod. "Not quite."

"Are you looking for one? I could set you up."

"You're winding me up."

"No. You're a good looking fellow. You need smartening up a little bit, maybe a cooked meal or two."

"I'm fine, thank you. I wouldn't want to put anyone through such an ordeal."

Ronda sipped her wine again. "Now why do you do that?"

"Do what?"

"Put yourself down like that."

"I was joking."

"I don't think you were."

"Say, what is this? You wouldn't happen to be a psychiatrist now, would you?"

"No, but if its Valium you're after, Apollo's got a hook-up."

"No, thank you. See this here?" I raised the Guinness. "That's all the anti-depressant that I need."

"Why won't you let me set you up?"

"Why are you so *desperate* to set me up?"

"I like watching love flourish."

I choked on the head of the Guinness with laughter. "Oh baby, you haven't got a clue, have you?"

"You're telling me you've never loved a woman before?"

I put the Guinness down and sighed.

"John Butler, I asked you a question..."

"My mother, I suppose."

Ronda thought for a moment. "How sweet."

I nodded.

"Is she still with us, your mother?"

"No."

"I'm sorry."

"I was too."

"You were close?"

"You could say that."

"And your father?"

A smell of Jameson's hit me in the nostrils. It was corrosive. I looked up quickly and saw the bar tender passing by with a tray of doubles.

"John Butler?"

"Yes."

"Your father?"

"What about him?"

"Were you close?"

"No."

"How so?"

"I suppose we were physically close at times. You have to be fairly close to kick the living shit out of someone, don't you?"

I hit the chick Ronda with some cold, hard truth. Maybe that would back her off. She acted stunned but I think it only ignited more of an interest in me.

I didn't like this.

I felt like I was being interrogated.

Worse.

Worse than a police interrogation about a crime.

The interrogation was about me, my life...

"I'm sorry to hear that."

"Don't be. It made me the man I am today."

"And is that a good thing?"

"I -," I opened my mouth, but no smart-arse response came out.

"Is your father still alive?"

"No, he's not."

"Has he been dead long?"

"Not long enough, as far as I'm concerned. I dig his coffin up every few weeks, just to check he's still in there."

Ronda forced a laugh. "Brothers and sisters?"

"Yeah."

"Are you close with them?"

"What do you think?"

I finished the Guinness and heard acoustic bass coming from the beer garden. Apollo would soon be clearing it of patrons, no doubt.

"I've experienced some of that myself," Ronda said.

"Oh?"

"You're not the only one, John Butler."

"I'm aware."

"I found that -,"

"Please, Ronda. You're a nice lady. I don't want to be rude."

"What do you mean?"

"I mean: let's change the subject, okay?"

"It's a sensitive topic for you, isn't it?"

"No shit."

"Talking can help."

"Babe, I've only just met you."

"And I've only just met you, but I can see a real sadness in you, John Butler. It's a shame. You have a nice smile, a genuine laugh, a pretty face. There's a real bluebird in your heart, but you're drowning it."

I liked the reference.

"Thanks, Ronda. You're very kind."

"Talk to me."

"Now why would I do that?"

"It helps. It helped me."

"We're not all the same."

"Try it."

"Fine!"

She gave a gentle sigh, like a political candidate that had just delivered a killer blow in a debate. "In your own time..."

"There's nothing to tell. Like you said, I'm no different to anyone else. My old man was a piece of shit. A drunk. A bully. He made our lives hell, first chance I got – I split."

"What did he do to you?"

"Whatever he felt like."

"And your mother?"

"My mother was an angel. And he..." I trailed off.

*Was I actually going to do this?*

I took a deep breath and wetted my whistle –

"Augustine Hassle, or Auggie to his friends, grew up on a dirt-poor farm in County Mayo somewhere. He moved to Birmingham, worked on sites as a groundworker, digging footings. He was a hard worker, wore out two hip replacements in trenches with his shovel. He met...charmed...married...and battered a pretty girl from Sligo into a creaking, gin-soaked, Catholic mess. Together Auggie and Clodagh had four children, two boys and two girls. Clodagh died of cancer and Auggie died of cirrhosis. Auggie's friends remember him as a hard worker who liked a drink, and his family try not to remember him at all."

Ronda had finished her wine.

"Happy?" I asked her and finished the pint.

"And your childhood?"

"Was mainly spent hiding. When I was fifteen, I left."

"Where did you go?"

"Nowhere in particular, anywhere that would put me up for the night."

"Are you the oldest sibling?"

"No, youngest."

"And you don't stay in touch with them?"

I laughed. "They're dead to me."

"Why would you say that?"

I smirked. "Every one of them went through it, put up with it, experienced it from the old man. They knew. They put up with it and they left, left me alone to go through it too."

"Maybe they were scared."

"Maybe I was fucking scared, did they think of that? They fucked off first chance they got and left me, alone, with that bastard, trying to protect mom and -,"

*What the hell was I doing?*

"I'm done," I told her.

"But you feel better from sharing?"

"Do I fuck. Now I've turned all this shit back on!" I hit my palm against the side of my head and aggressively signalled the bar tender for another Guinness.

"John Butler, if you ever need to talk, I am here."

"Thanks, Ronda. I think you've done enough."

"Sharing can -,"

"Babe, enough."

A bell sounded –

It was deafening –

Terrifying –

The lights came on –

Blinding –

Jolting –

And he was stood there –

At the back of the bar –

Holding a glass –

Clenching a fist –

Dead eyes –

Looking at me –

I jumped up from the table and took off.

"John Butler!" I heard Ronda call after me.

I stumbled past the champagne socialists and heard muffled laughter follow me. Then I fell out the door. Fell out from the bright, burning clarity of The Fighting Cocks into the dark littered shadows of the Moseley streets.

In the darkness I was safe again.

## 36

The darkness never frightened me. Never. I think I was made in it, or my soul was, wherever souls are made. Some of the darkness that surrounded its birth found its way inside. I was comfortable in it because I was of it. It offered safety, it offered escape, hiding, protection – all the things that light took away. The light was what terrified me. I feared the daylight, the sun, naked flames, lightbulbs swinging from ceilings... The light lays everything bare and illuminates all. The daylight shows all your scars, all your scars for all to see. The ones on your flesh, and others, deeper, worser scars, scars on your soul, that sometime a face can allude to and reveal. You can see fear in a man's eyes. It's as prevalent as brown or blue. The fear tells things, stories, of their past, about locked cupboards, about belts, about uncles, about things, all the things humankind are capable of.

Back at the Rowton I was drinking whiskey neat in the darkness.

I was struggling to see the glass to pour.

Turning the light on never occurred to me.

"The dumb bitch," I said to whatever ghouls surrounded me in the onyx of my room.

"Well, that's not entirely fair..."

"True, I think she was trying to help."

"But she doesn't know what she's done."

"Yup... uncorked the whole fucking thing."

"Everyday."

"Every moment."

"You're holding it together, aren't you?"

"I'm trying so hard."

"And the do-gooders, with their hand holding and their bullshit..."

"Thanks a lot, Ronda!"

I was thinking about my mother now.

I should have been thinking about Val Vulva. I should have been thinking about his poor mother. I should have been preparing myself for the next night, The Midnight Special, The Gulldongs and Theo Oak and the danger to life.

*But no!*

Instead, the figure in the darkness before me was of an elderly lady. Self-inflicted cripple. A handbag by her hip, her hair tied up, a dress below her knees. The silhouette swayed gently by the door to the bathroom. I watched it. It said nothing. It smelt familiar, of overcooked meat - gammon, a burn of gin and incense from mass.

"Mother..."

She was all around me now.

I hit a double hard and refilled.

My dear, old mother.

She had been dead long before the day she died.

He saw to that.

And when she was in that bed, crippled by those fucking tumours, she still made me do it. Down to the shop, up that fucking isle, collect that fucking bottle. Every trip - less tonic, less tonic, until none...

That was his gift to her.

His disease.

His misery.

That was an awful time. By that point you could smell the cancer on her breath.

And even though the old man was gone, he still hung around in all the strife. When sorrow spawned, he lay within it.

"I hope you burn forever," I said and willed his ghost to hear me.

I was never like any of my family, especially those that still hung around. I detested them. I hated the Catholic masochism of them all. How they suffered, how they tolerated abuse, struggling on with a glum smile. They got off on it. They made me sick. Martyrs. Suffering and loving to be seen suffering, it was almost as if they tried to outdo each other with how dreadful their lives were. They were pathetic. They never attempted to better themselves and they never showed any guts. They ate shit and thanked each other for it. That was the problem with Martyrs, from history until today – they're all gutless losers. It doesn't take any bottle to let someone nail you to a piece of wood. It takes bottle to go down fighting, swing your sword, or your fist, die with honour, not a snivelling, submissive coward. A hero. A dead hero. But a hero all the same.

I shocked them to death at mom's funeral. Anthony showed up, my older brother. He was in a state, and they all gave him a few quid. He walked up to me, and I told him to *do one*. I heard the sanctimonious gasps and saw the theatrical shock from all the biddies and their downtrodden husbands. Aunts, uncles, cousins, whatever... *cunts*, I would group them as.

"Don't be like that, Paddy," he'd slurred at me.

"Fuck you," I'd said.

A Hail Mary to keep mom happy, and then I was gone.

I'd never see them again.

I burnt my bridges, so I had to learn to swim.

"Fine with me."

I was happier in the water with the sharks anyway.

The old man's funeral had been harder. I was younger then, impressionable and foolish. It was so damn hard to act like I wasn't over-the-moon that he was dead. I tried to show decorum and hang my head.

*Can you believe I actually carried the fucker in?*

I should have thrown him in a fucking dumpster.

(But even the council wouldn't have taken that bastard.)

The picture they'd put on his casket still haunted me.

He was smiling. I'd never seen him smile. Somehow the smile scared me more than when he grinded his teeth and lost it. It was creepy. *What was he smiling at? What makes a demon smile?* And his eyes... Jesus. I'd seen more life in glass eyes than in his.

Then again, there was a certain class to it. God forbid the photographs that would be placed on the caskets of my generation. Photoshopped, filtered Facebook profile photos from years ago – nothing like the person, before death or at any point in their life, stupid fake eyes, air-brushed skin to hide the spots, pouting, pouting like a tit. At least the old man's had class – black and white, suit, Ted haircut – how it should be.

"But that's enough about all this!" I said out loud.

I heard a crash and I'd knocked the whiskey over.

"Bollocks!"

I tried to pick it up and dropped my cigarette.

The carpet caught fire.

"TAE FUCK WITH YA!"

In my drunken state, rather than just using water from the sink in the bathroom, I left my room and rushed down to the icebox in the hall. I collected two fistfuls of ice and ran back to my room...

But the door had locked, and I didn't have the key.

"TAAAAEEE FUUUUUCK WITH YAAAAA!"

I rushed downstairs to the receptionist. I was barefoot and the two handfuls of ice were melting in my hands. She looked stunned -

"Mr Bundy! Whatever is the matter?"

Just as I opened my mouth to speak –

The fire alarm went off.

"My room! I've locked myself out."

"Oh my god... FIRE!" she shrieked.

"No, no. There's a small, contained fire in my room, nothing to worry about. Could you let me back in?"

We ran back up the stairs.

"What is going on?" she asked me.

"I was having a party."

"A party?"

*What are you talking about, Hassle?*

"Yes, erm, an Easter party."

*Easter? It's January, you prick!*

When we got to the room she unlocked the door, opened it, and stared in at a smouldering carpet and the entire absence of any other person.

*"A party?"*

"Goodnight."

I went inside and shut the door.

It was time for bed.

## 37

Wythall was a suburb on the outskirts of Birmingham. It was bordering rural country, so was mainly full of white flighters from the inner city, people escaping the lunatics who were making their lives hell. It was a strange place. An overspill. Not exactly country and not exactly city, just an inbred cousin of them both.

There was an offie by the train station, so I parked my car up, grabbed twenty Chesterfields and a couple of tins of Holsten. I put one tin in my jacket pocket, cracked the other and meandered down the path to the station.

At first, I thought I'd got the wrong date or time.

It was silent and seemed abandoned.

But when I reached the bottom of the path, I saw about fifty or so young kids, all stood quietly, well-dressed and stinking of wealth.

They must have been under strict instructions to remain quiet until the train arrived, probably to deter drawing attention to the illegal party.

I sipped at my lager and studied them -

They were kids from Dickens Heath, Earlswood, so on and so on. The path leading further out of Birmingham towards Stratford-upon-Avon, and all the rich little white villages in between. These snobs had fathers that voted Tory, drove Jaguars, and cycled in lycra on weekends. Their mothers paid extortionate amounts of money for garden furniture and flew annually abroad so that Turks could modify their faces and arses. Plastic faces. Faces like fascia board. And wanker fathers. Fat, brandy-swilling wankers. I hated them. I hated their children. I hated them the same way I hated the Bolsheviks in Moseley, but at least the Moseley Bolsheviks were harmless. These kids had a cruel tinge in their white-toothed grins, and their walnut eyes. They looked like they thrill-killed homeless people on weekends, high on designer drugs, then posted it on their Instagrams. Get them drunk and their land baron ancestry would come spilling out – flog the serf, savage the women, steal the turnip crops.

A few more of them arrived and stood too close to me.

"I don't like anyone near me," I told to them, and they walked away immediately.

I represented what they feared –

A drunken paddy.

A crazed mick.

A potato picker with a grudge.

They were fake. They were phony... from their teeth to their hair, to their tans and their happiness. They were delusion. And I was reality. I was Barnes in Platoon. I was Hassle in Wythall.

Here stood an Irish son-of-a-gun with nothing to lose.

They had plenty to lose. Their front teeth, for starters.

And no orthodontist in East Anglia would be able to correct the damage Hassle could do, not even if *daddy* splashed out big-time and *mommy* only got the one arse-cheek done.

My semi-outburst telling them to *back off* seemed to give the rest of the snobs on the platform some confidence. They started chatting in groups, giggling, bragging, sniggering and drinking – alcopops or top shelf liquor...

Top shelf liquor mixed with value cola? That made no sense to me.

They all sounded southern, even though they weren't.

Something about the south and entitled richness just ran parallel.

They were all the children of thieves. Descendants of the Norman rapists and marauders who had invaded the Anglo-Saxon natives in 1066. The wealth they had and the land they claimed – it was all stolen. It wasn't theirs. And the racism and nationalism that they harboured was laughable. It was a joke. Why? Because *they* were the immigrants. *They* were the foreigners. *They* had stolen the jobs, stolen the money and took up the space... *Give me masses of Polish bricklayers or Bangladeshi shop owners any day, over these entitled French thieves!*

"Urgh," I shivered. The hatred coursing through me was beginning to make me ill.

I'd had enough of studying the snobs.

The safari was making me nauseous.

I wandered away and sparked a Chesterfield.

The nicotine would calm me down, I decided.

I walked right down to the end of the platform, in the darkness and alone.

All that accompanied me was a sign with a number and a slogan: *Don't do it. Talk to us.* It was a suicide hotline.

These stations usually had a high suicide rate. The trains didn't stop as often and passed through at high speeds.

It didn't seem like a good death to me –

Being torn apart by a train.

But I supposed if you detached your thoughts from what would happen to your body, and what you'd look like afterwards, then it would be quick and painless.

I wondered how many people had stood alone by the sign, like me.

I wondered how many had called the number and been saved.

And I wondered how many had ignored it, not seen it, considered it, but done it anyway...

I walked back up the platform and opened the second tin of Holsten.

The crowd had grown bigger and more repulsive.

For the first time I noticed a sign hung on the side of the platform shelter -

It was advertising some kind of live cooking event in Birmingham city centre. The picture of the chef was terrifying.

He was bald and smiling, but he was *too bald* and *too smiling*. He had glasses on, thick-rimmed glasses, but they didn't seem like his. Instead, I imagined they belonged to a deceased family member, and he wore them to suppress some horrid memory about LSD and a hot press. He looked like a gay serial killer. Like if he dropped his arse, it would smell of a dead homosexual in a bath – as well as a dirty oven.

The tagline below him read: *Cooking with spice!*

"More like, cooking *on* spice," I cleverly joked to myself.

Spice was a craze among the degenerates of Birmingham. It was synthetic cannabis, but unlike cannabis, which just chilled or cabbaged the user out, spice instead seemed to paralyse them. It was fascinating, the first few times I'd seen it. Then it proved to be annoying. The tramps that smoked it experienced all their muscles and joints locking up. When you passed them, they seemed frozen in time, either mid-stride, or hunched over about to puke. It was like a frozen PS2 game, called *Scumbag* or something.

"He looks like he's on spice," I motioned at the chef and prodded a toff who stood near to me.

He turned and looked, then looked at me – bewildered.

The toff walked away.

They had no sense of humour.

As I glugged at the can, I noticed two bright lights.

They were coming up from the darkness, from the end of the platform by the suicide sign.

The time had come -

The Midnight Special was arriving.

## 38

The train looked like any other, a green and yellow public train, they ran hundreds of times a day across Birmingham and here was just another. Only it wasn't just another – it had pulled up into a station it shouldn't have and at a time that it shouldn't have.

There was an ominous quiet pause on the platform as the train halted and the doors opened.

Wind was picking up on the platform and so too was excitement. Stars in the sky were dancing, leaves were gusting past us and I too, although present for professional reasons, was feeling a buzz of excitement.

We formed queues, and soon, I was stepping inside...

The walls were studded out and sound-proofed, and the carriages were in complete darkness.

Everyone piled in.

We were like sardines. (Or maybe monkfish? Considering the wealth of those stuffed together.)

When everyone climbed aboard the doors shut.

Silence.

And then –

"Ladies and gentlemen..." a voice began over the tannoy. It was a well-spoken voice. Perfect English, with the remnants of a Birmingham accent hidden somewhere. "Welcome to The Midnight Special..." I wondered if it was my faceless nemesis – Theo Oak?

A roar exploded inside the carriage.

Lights began to dance, every colour, every speed. It was epilepsy on coke. It was mayhem. The toffs threw back their heads, sunk their drinks and became intoxicated on the pheromones, the testosterone and the adrenaline that bonded together into some primeval cocktail within the carriage walls.

I needed space.

I pushed through bodies, male and female, warm and alien. I pushed forwards and got to the end of the carriage.

I slid the door ahead of me open and moved on into another –

This one was less crowded.

This carriage had walls that were cladded in oak. It was classy. There were leather seats at precarious positions, not laid out in the communist West Midlands transport style. Soft jazz, possibly Chet Baker, was playing, and people were ordering drinks at a big bar.

I joined them, hooked my foot on the brass and waited –

This was my kind of carriage.

As I waited, I gazed out of the train window –

We were passing through Shirley, another Birmingham suburb, heading back for the city centre.

Every so often I caught sight of kids, under-aged teens frustrated in their bedrooms. They were looking out of their windows, dreaming of drunkenness, freedom and sin. They saw the train and their eyes lit up. (Their parents would never believe them the next morning.)

Finally, I got served. They didn't have Holsten, so I got a pint of Star. It was strong Czech beer. It tasted good and it was free. *A free bar?* I was in heaven. God knows how much a ticket on The Midnight Special must have been.

"In that case, buddy," I leant forward. "Gimmie a Johnny Walker Blue, make it a double."

He nodded and without hesitation served me a double of one of the most expensive whiskeys in the country.

It tasted like tree bark and moonlight.

"HASS! HASS!"

I jumped and raised my fists – but it was Patrice.

His eyelids were stapled open by amphetamines. And his pupils were like magic eight balls. Shake them and they'd say: *You're going to get fucked up...*

"How're you doing, Patrice?" I shook his hand.

"Want a livener?"

"No. I'm working."

"So you'll work quicker then?"

"Again, no."

"What d'you think, man? *The Midnight Special!*"

"Well, it sure is something."

"We did a soundcheck at Danzey station, dude. You ever been there? It's just fields, bro. Boring-ass fields. Anyway, we sound-checked at half-ten at night, can you believe that? Some farmer motherfucker came over to tell us to be quiet and someone shot him."

*"Shot him?"*

"Yeah, full of horse tranquilisers."

"That's sick."

"I know right – awesome!"

"Whatever you say, Patrice."

"Want to come and say hello to the rest of the guys?"

I needed to find Theo Oak.

He was what I had come for.

But I also needed to stay casual and not raise suspicion.

"Yeah, all right."

Patrice led the way.

We passed through carriage after carriage –

Each one had its own theme in terms of music and décor -

There was Indie. (The music was lemon. The people wore check shirts, had small hands and would have been useless in a fight.)

There was drum n' bass. (Everyone was completely out of control from the intoxicating thudding of the music and the powerful drugs they'd just dropped moments before.)

There was a Reggae and Jungle kind of room. (At first, I thought there was a dry ice machine in there, but no...)

Another was full of pilled-up ravers. (They were all in UV with UV paint on their face, sweating and half-naked, dancing like python women and iguana men. It was erotic and terrifying and repulsive all at the same time.)

Eventually and drunkenly, I found myself staggering through a carriage door and into the open air.

The VIP, or Green Room carriage, was open topped.

It had a mesh kind of grid for a ceiling and was full of the artists who would be performing later, organisers, villains, heavies and members of staff.

(*Here Comes My Baby* by *The Tremeloes* was playing.)

Patrice led me across to the rest of The Gulldongs.

"How're you doing, Hass," Hopper said, and we shook hands.

"I'm fine, Hopper. Just fine."

Scratch Man nodded at me.

Violence was always on my mind. So, I asked about something that had been bugging me –

"Where're all the bouncers? I haven't seen any."

"There's only one," Patrice gurned at me.

"*One?* For all that lot?" I motioned with my thumb back to the door. "There's hundreds of people. And they're all drugged-up and mental."

"Trust me, Hass," Hopper said. "You haven't seen him."

"Crumblemeat," Patrice said.

"Excuse me?"

"That's his name, bro. Crumblemeat."

"That's not a fucking name."

"No, no, no," Hopper tried to interject with some common sense. "He is a professional wrestler. His *wrestling name* is Crumblemeat."

"He's big, Hassle! Big!"

"Supposedly his trick is…" Hopper began. "To do a line of cocaine off a twenty-five-kilo weight plate. He pinches it between two fingers, then snorts the line with the other hand."

"What kind of trick is that?" I asked.

"Awesome," Patrice nodded.

"Well, only to be shown at very selective parties," I added.

They all agreed.

"He works for Oak, man," Patrice carried on. "He's on suspension from wrestling for breaking a dude's neck in the ring. They reckon he done it on purpose."

Cogs turned within my head...

Wrestler? Theo Oak enforcer? And neck-snapping-prowess?

*Had I finally stumbled across Val Vulva's killer?*

Here I had a suspect – but I needed a confession or DNA evidence to link him to the murder.

"You okay, Hassle?" Hopper asked me.

I awoke from my daydream. "Yes. Yes. I'm fine."

"You look trippy, man. Are you on the shrooms, dude?" Patrice asked.

"What do you think?"

He just looked at me and laughed.

"What's with this beat music anyway?" I asked.

"Oh, that's Theo," Hopper answered.

Scratch Man suddenly screamed (and was ignored).

"No, That's *The Tremeloes*."

"I mean he's into the sixties stuff."

"Oh, I see," I nodded.

"You don't tell Theo what to play in his own green room, bro," added Patrice.

I couldn't fault Oak's taste in music.

While The Gulldongs began to chatter among themselves about their setlist and the afterparty, I lit a Chesterfield and turned around. I scanned across the faces in the VIP carriage and locked onto one in particular. Before I could think, Patrice confirmed a suspicion –

"That's Theo, dude."

He looked like the bareknuckle gypsy brother of Clark Gable.

Crooked nose with a pencil-thin moustache, scar-tissue eyes with a shining smile. His hair was slicked back, black, and shiny. He was over six-feet tall and wearing an old school pinstripe, Roaring Twenties style. He was puffing on a Cuban.

"Looks classy," I said to Patrice.

"Theo is the man."

Oak was talking to a bunch of people.

One of them separated from the conversation and started coming right at me.

I readied myself.

"Hi fellas," the man said.

He looked about the same age as The Gulldongs but dressed differently. He was wearing a woolly jumper in childish colours and had a pair of expensive designer glasses perched on his nose.

When I glanced back to Oak, I saw he was leaving.

"Hello, Junior," I heard Hopper say from behind me.

I whispered to Patrice –

"Who's this?"

"Junior. He's Oak's son."

Junior was sipping WKD and still grinning. Two girls joined him, and they looked about fourteen years old. I didn't approve.

"Who are these?" I asked Junior and motioned at the girls.

"Erm, what?" he stuttered.

"Are these your sisters?"

All three of them laughed.

"No, no, no," Junior shrugged. "We're just friends..." he hooked an arm around the hips of them both. (I didn't share blood with either of the girls, but I felt suddenly defensive.) "Anyway, we're going to check out the music," Junior took a swig of WKD and wandered away with them both. (He'd just made my shit-list.)

"What was that all about?" I asked Patrice.

He pulled a strange face and shrugged at me.

"Oak's son can do what he wants, I suppose," Hopper tried to explain.

My mind reverted back to business –

Oak –

Oak Sr. –

Follow him –

I collected a ticket off Patrice, thanked him and followed in the direction that Oak had left.

I opened the carriage door and found myself in a heavy-metal room. It was fairly empty, seeing as the genre was not one too popular with spoilt rich kids.

However, for the first time, I got to lay my eyes on Crumblemeat –

The Gulldongs hadn't been exaggerating. He was enormous. A giant. If the rich kids on The Midnight Special were the descendants of Norman thieves, then Crumblemeat was the descendent of the Viking raiders that had come before them. He must have been an easy six-foot six, twenty odd stone. He had a bleach-blond mullet, thick black moustache and eyes that were too close together – the number one sign of a psycho.

When he approached me, he looked as though he was staring at a well-done steak, not another human.

"Ticket," he grumbled.

I handed it to him, and he stamped it.

Then he barged through me, sending me staggering to one side.

*It's him!* A voice seemed to bellow from inside me. Or maybe it came from the night air outside. Maybe it was Val, giving me a hint from beyond the grave.

The man just stunk of death. I was certain he was a killer. Was he the killer I was after? Well, he sure fit the bill. He was big enough and skilled enough to kill a pathetic, little junkie like Val Vulva. He was also an Oak enforcer.

I needed evidence.

I needed to keep cool.

No way I'd be able to get a confession out of the monster. I couldn't intimidate him or beat it out of him. Apollo was right. I needed to be smart, not gung-ho.

If I could get some of his DNA, then that could be enough to link Crumblemeat to the murder scene. But how the hell was I going to do that? And without revealing myself? If I got identified as Paddy Hassle, I was as good as dead.

I ordered another Star, this time from the bar in the heavy metal room.

The music was loud and aggressive –

*R.A.M.O.N.E.S.* by *Motorhead.*

But it helped me think.

I came up with a vague plan, necked the beer and headed into the next carriage.

As I stepped through the door, I felt the train beginning to slow down.

I looked out of the window and saw we were arriving at Snow Hill Train Station.

Snow Hill was a main station in Birmingham city centre. I was impressed when I saw the emptiness of the place – no staff, no drunkards, no homeless bedding down for the night. Oak had actually managed to commandeer the whole station – this took some doing.

But then something else caught my attention –

A group of people waiting on the platform.

They weren't rich kids.

No way.

I could tell that immediately.

They looked rough, and they were all dressed in high-vis vests.

When we got nearer, I saw the vests had things written on them:

*Cocaine.*

*MDMA.*

*Ketamine.*

They were all dealers! Dealers that had uniforms!

Oak had run this like a military operation. (Once again, I was impressed.)

Anticipation was in the air as the train grinded to a halt. The rich kids were like dogs on heat, salivating for their sedation or stimulation. I, however, was uninterested. The queue at the bar was shorter, so I ordered two more pints and sunk them –

Dutch courage and obligation.

Those were my reasons.

"Another!" I demanded, banging a fist on the bar.

The barman obliged with another pint of Czech's finest.

I stayed back and watched, like any true investigator.

Humans interested me. They pissed me off, mostly, but I found their behaviours interesting. I had been an observer of their behaviour for most of my life, I got to know it well, their vices and how to manipulate and use them.

The dealer who had *Spice* written on his high-vis was particularly terrifying. He looked like a Centaur. His back must have been broken badly and not properly mended, because his arse and his legs were offset a foot or so behind him. He also had a George Cross tattoo on his forehead that had faded. In truth to the bloke, if you showed me a picture of him, I'd have picked *spice dealer* as his job before anything else. He was living the dream. The spice dealing dream. Fair play to him. Fair play, indeed.

The Czech lager was fuelling me with unleaded energy.

A good plan involving Oak and Crumblemeat was concocting inside my head.

Then the voice on the tannoy started again -

"Ladies and gentlemen... Please feel free to indulge in the various products now on sale. Enjoy..."

The voice...it tasted like ivory.

It just had to be Oak.

But enough of that –

I needed to get on with my plan!

So I approached one of the dealers – the *MDMA* one.

"What can I do you?" he asked me.

"A baggy, kid. And now!"

"How much?"

"Just the baggy."

"A baggy?"

"Yes, damn it. The baggy! The baggy!"

He shook his head. "How much do you want, you drunk fuck?"

"You're not listening, are you punk? I just want the baggy."

"Empty?"

"Yes."

"Why?"

"Jesus Christ, do you ask every customer *why?*"

"It'll cost you."

"What? For an empty fucking baggy?"

"Shit yes."

"How much?"

He thought for a second. "Twenty-five pence."

"Get to fuck."

"Twenty-five pence or no baggy."

"You'll be a millionaire one day, trust me," I grumbled.

I looked in my wallet. "Shit."

"What?"

"Would you take twenty?"

He sighed. "I suppose."

"Just give me the fucking thing!"

I gave him twenty pence and took my empty baggy.

*Man, that seemed harder than it had to be!*

I put the empty baggy in my pocket and started moving through the train. I kept going, pushing, gliding, around drunks, dancers, dealers, delinquents. My senses were keen, my eyes were sharp. I was on the lookout for Oak – and then I finally found him.

His Cuban was almost finished.

He was grinning and slapping some kid on the back.

The kid looked like a complete dickhead. He was wearing a mustard-coloured shirt, undone to show his amazing tan. He also had on chino shorts and some loafers with no socks.

I assumed Oak, cold-blooded gangster, was using the kid or the kid's father in some way. The kid's father probably laundered money for Oak (or something of the sort).

I followed him stealthily as he left the kid and went into a bathroom.

I went in behind him.

We were alone.

He was taking a piss, heaving the last few drags on the Cuban.

I readied myself –

Then I opened my mouth –

"Evening."

I noticed the muscles in Oak's back and legs tense up. I had startled him and his street smarts, like that of a seasoned alley cat, had him on edge.

He looked over his shoulder at me. "Help you?"

(His voice matched that on the tannoy.)

"We've got a friend in common."

He sneered, uninterested. "Oh, and who's that?"

"John Stod."

The sound of urine splashing against porcelain ceased.

Oak composed himself, reached into his breast pocket and produced another cigar. He zipped himself up, lit the Cuban and then turned to face his enemy.

"So… you're that fucking drunken detective, huh?"

"Fuckin' A."

"That loser from Moseley?"

"I wouldn't say that exactly."

"That stupid fucking dipshit P.I., whose fucking everything up?"

"Sounds more like it."

Stod smirked at me, then puffed cigar smoke across the bathroom. "You've got some sack, coming here. I'll give you that."

"I've come here for one reason."

"Oh yeah?"

"Yeah. I'm giving yous one chance to turn yourselves in. Clear my name and admit what you've done."

He laughed at me – loud and obnoxious. "Why would I do that?"

"To save us both a lot of trouble. You see… both you and Stod don't have the foggiest idea who you're messing with. I might be a drunk. Fuck it, I might be a loser. But I live for this shit."

"And you think I don't?" he grinned at me.

"You smug shitheel. I'll wipe that smile off your face."

"*Will you?*"

It was my turn to laugh at him. "Okay. Let's see then, *Theo*…"

"Yes, let's…"

I smiled at him, then I let myself out of the bathroom.

"I'll be seeing you," I winked.

"Oh, you will," he winked back.

I shut the door behind me and picked up my pace.

Almost instantly, and over the sound of music and shouting, I heard it open behind me.

Oak was after me.

"Hey…" I heard his voice.

*Move it, Hassle!*

"HEY!"

People in the carriage looked, but I kept facing forwards and kept moving.

In front of me, blocking my escape, was that dickhead kid who was talking to Oak before he went for a piss.

"Excuse me!" he stuck his hand out to stop me.

I stopped.

"Theo Oak is a *personal* friend of mine," he started. "He and my father go way back, and if you dare insult or -,"

I punched him as hard as I could in the face and watched him vomit his teeth through his nose.

He fell into a heap of mustard shirt, loafers and blood.

The rest of the carriage cleared the way for me.

"HEY!" Oak called again.

I ran into the next carriage, pushing through dancing druggies, not knowing where I was going or how to escape.

*Was this it?*

*Was this the end?*

*Would I not live to see another hangover?*

The carriage was packed.

I looked into the mass of rich, spoilt flesh - the toffs, the snobs, the rich kids. I thought about their Audis, their partings, their chinos, their drugs and their wealth. Then I thought about my friends in Moseley, even the Bolsheviks! The penniless, the Audiless... The only thing my mates had in ample supply was *nothing*. I was enraged. I thought about Val Vulva. I thought about how these rich bastards would have laughed at him, how they would have thought of him as nothing but dirt -

Then I went berserk.

"TORY BASTARDS!"

I tore through the crowd with my fists. I lashed out at anything that moved. I hit shoulders, breasts, hair and ears. Anything. Anything that moved. The men moaned like women and the women moaned like men. These rich, inbred Conservatives were a depraved bunch, so I took pleasure with each connection of flesh to flesh.

At the end of the carriage, I stopped to catch my breath –

I turned around -

Oak was looking at me from the other end –

And he had Crumblemeat at his side.

"Get him, Meat!" Oak said and pointed a finger at me.

Crumblemeat smiled. He'd been waiting for an excuse to commit some random violence – and now he'd found it.

He started striding down the carriage -

Big, Nordic strides -

I had to time this perfectly -

I readied myself -

I got into a fighting stance -

He was getting nearer -

Pushing people out of his way –

Nearer -

I could smell him -

Smell the anger -

The murder -

The danger -

He was close -

Closer -

Ready -

*Hassle?* -

Get ready...

And...

NOW!

Just as he extended two arms to grab me, I slammed Putlog into his face as hard as I could. I summoned all the strength from my forefathers, the ditch-diggers, the potato-pickers, the railway-builders, all my disgruntled mick ancestry.

Crumblemeat collapsed to one knee.

*Jesus Christ…*

I'd never seen anyone take a blow from Putlog like that before.

And he wasn't really hurt –

Just stunned.

*Quickly, Hassle!*

I took the empty baggy from inside my leather jacket.

Then I grabbed hold of Crumblemeat's big bulldog head and jammed a thumb into his mouth.

"PERVERT! PERRRRVERRRT!" someone started screaming.

I took the moist thumb back out and rubbed it off inside the baggy. Then pulled a clump of blond mullet hair for good measure.

Crumblemeat DNA. *Bingo!*

I looked up and saw shock on Theo Oak's face -

I smiled -

Crumblemeat shook his head and began waking up -

I rushed over to the train door -

We were still moving -

The night, light and frights of Birmingham were still whizzing past the door, but it was my only escape –

I grabbed the handle and started wrenching it open -

Theo Oak was running down the carriage -

"Don't let him go, Meat!" he was shouting -

Crumblemeat was standing, holding his jaw and lunging for me –

But it was too late –

I got the door open -

"Goodbye, motherfuckers!" I yowled as I disappeared into a midnight blur -

I hit the floor hard -

I rolled a few times -

My ribs got bashed-up -

My lip split open -

And my ankle twisted -

And at that moment, I didn't think things could get any worse.

Then I looked up at the sign to tell me where I was –

Small Heath.

"Ah, fuck."

# 39

I limped my way through Small Heath, down to the scrapyard by the arches. My ankle was in a bad way, and each step seemed to pump the swelling up more and more.

Eventually a people carrier pulled up beside me. An old Muslim bloke was driving, a devout bloke, with all the gear on.

"Are you okay, my son?" he asked.

What a gent.

He drove me all the way back to Wythall station to collect my car.

"Here's fine," I kept saying, pointing to wherever we were. "I'll walk the rest."

"No problem, no problem," he repeated.

He wouldn't accept any cash in return for his kindness.

So I stole his debit card instead. (I needed it to find his sort code and account number.) I transferred him one hundred quid and posted the card back to an address I'd managed to bleed out of him during the journey.

The Juara was still standing.

The backseats were shitless.

And the screen wash was full.

I slipped inside, turned on the heaters and felt myself begin to relax.

I checked the doors –

Locked.

I sorted the music –

*Return To Sender* came on from shuffle.

I was happy with that.

There was a warm can of Holsten in the glove compartment, so I cracked it and giggled merrily to the music.

The King provided the soundtrack to my drive back to Digbeth, and back to the Rowton hotel.

I used the lifts to get up to my room, then I had a hot shower and fell into bed.

The room was dark.

I was tired but content.

Things were finally going in Hassle's favour, like they always did.

I had evidence.

I had DNA.

And I had a story – my story – the truth.

It wasn't perfect.

But it was getting there.

# 40

I awoke the next morning and left my room quickly. The toothpaste had run out, so I smoked a menthol instead from a pack I kept in my toiletries for emergencies. It did the job.

I wandered around Digbeth again, but this time was smooth enough to avoid St Anne's and the Sunday service kick-out.

I caught a number 50 bus. Not for any reason, just for something to do. I sat at the back on the top and drank a can of beer. I wanted solitude – but someone joined me and it escalated quickly.

"I'm telling you man, heroin helped me quit drinking!" he said.

Whenever I sat on a bus and drank a can, nutters used it as an excuse to strike up conversation. Like we were brothers in debauchery. We weren't... well, at least I hoped we weren't.

Then suddenly I recognised the particular nutter -

"Hang on, I thought you didn't use heroin?" I asked.

He looked shocked.

"Yeah, you're the bloke who works on the cranes!" I said.

He stood up. "No, that wasn't me!"

"Yeah, it was!" I chased after him. "You lied!"

The nutter started pointing at me and shouting to the other passengers. "That man is mental! Totally mental!"

He staggered down the stairs and I sat back down.

People looked at me. Their faces said –

*If THAT bloke is calling you mental, then you must have serious problems.*

I got off the bus and walked around aimlessly.

I found a pub on Bradford Street called The Anchor.

It was old school.

I walked inside and asked the bartender for a pint of the black stuff. I watched it settle in a daydream, then I took it across to a seat by the pool table.

A couple of blokes were shooting pool.

One of them seemed better than the other.

One of them lost.

But neither of them cared.

They were both drunk.

And winning didn't matter.

They both already were.

For the first time since I'd stumbled across that kid's body, I was feeling good. I wasn't feeling like a rat in a cage anymore, being walked across to a dustbin full of water. No, no, no. I'd sunk my teeth into the executioner's fingers, the cage had dropped, lid broken, and off I'd scurried into the weeds and the brambles.

A man was drinking a glass of wine in the corner of the pub.

I wanted to shout at him - *Wine? You ponce!*

(No self-respecting man should drink wine in public. No way. And the problem isn't in the liquid itself – it's in the glass! There's no dignified way for a man to hold it. Not without looking like a boy-hungry Tory.)

As I sipped the Guinness (a well poured Guinness, I might add), I tried to think up what to do next...

I had the evidence on my laptop that I'd got from Stod's home. I had proof he was planning, or at least aware, of Val Vulva's murder. Oak was mentioned throughout these documents. I also had the DNA of Crumblemeat – the possible killer.

But even after all that –

It didn't seem like enough.

*What if Crumblemeat wasn't the killer?*

*What if it was all just coincidence?*

*Then I had fuck all!*

I had some documents that I'd *stolen* during a *break-in*. In fact, if I was wrong, then all I'd done was get myself involved in a lot more crimes and lengthened the list of charges I would be read.

"Confidence, Hassle! Confidence!" I assured myself, drinking and feeling the Guinness's foam French-kiss my moustache.

*Moustache?*

I put my Guinness down and told the pool sharks to guard it with their lives.

They laughed and agreed.

I went to the bathroom and admonished myself in the mirror:

"Good god, man. The state of you!"

I looked like a Venetian beggar.

My facial hair had always withered in strength in all areas but the moustache. My moustache was dense, like lead. After certain week-long binges without shaving, I'd noticed the envied stares of hipster kids who yearned to grow one as great as mine. But they couldn't. They couldn't grow a tumour, let alone a proper moustache.

Suddenly I heard a struggle from inside the toilet cubicle.

"Help! Help!" someone was screaming in terror.

"What?" I asked.

"HELP! HELP!"

I left the bathroom.

The pool sharks seemed to have guarded my drink well.

(I considered for a moment that maybe the Guinness was now laced with some kind of buggery-drug, but the thought didn't concern me for long.)

I finished the Guinness and had a second one.

"Would you like to put a song on?" the bartender asked me.

I thought for a moment. "I don't know."

"Well, if you do, just use your phone..." he explained something about an app that I had to download.

I half-listened, but mainly watched my Guinness. I willed the warring brown armies in the glass to separate into black and white, so they could both be devoured equally – without prejudice.

I sat down and messed about on my phone.

I wondered if liberals drank Guinness before it settled - because a settled Guinness was segregationist and racist.

Then I somehow downloaded the app successfully.

"What song?" I asked myself.

*Whip It* by *DEVO* was my choice.

This was good, I decided. This was good for me. To let off some steam and let my adrenaline catch some shut eye before the next surge.

"Hello, good sir," a gentleman in a Trilby hat said to me.

"Hello."

I watched him walk across to the bar and order a drink in a strange white jug.

I liked The Anchor. It had character.

But I needed another piss. So, I asked the pool sharks to guard my Guinness again, then I walked into the men's room.

I stood at the urinal and let it loose, just like the Stones did.

The cubicle was now silent.

"Life is good," I grinned to myself.

I decided I would return to Moseley.

I had the evidence.

I had the truth.

But mostly I had the faith.

The faith that the police would come to the right decision, do the rest of the leg work, unearth the other truths and disprove the other lies...

They would soon drag Stod and Oak and Crumblemeat away, hand them down some heavy sentences, and then give me some commendation or monetary award.

"Yeah...some fucking bread would be nice!" I shouted while I shook myself.

As I zipped up, ready to finish the Guinness and head home, my phone buzzed.

I pulled it out –

It was a message from an unknown number on WhatsApp –

I opened it up –

It was a video –

I pressed play...

There was a man screaming. Other figures were moving around. The camera was shaking. I didn't like it. I couldn't figure out what was happening. Who was hurting who? And what was going on?

Then the director finally steadied his camera...


Apollo was tied to a chair.

And they were burning his legs with clothes irons.

# 41

Leaving The Anchor was a blur. I felt black-out drunk, but drunk on terror. Terror and disbelief.

I rewatched the short clip, eleven seconds long, maybe five or six times in the drizzle on the Bradford Street pavement.

It was real. It wasn't fake.

They had my friend. And they were torturing him.

I grinded my teeth together. I felt the whites of my eyes cloud up like potato starch. He was in me again, always in me, radiating from inside. But sometimes I needed him. I hated to admit it. I hated him. Everything about him. But I needed his venom and his wrath. Now I needed him more than ever!

"Get ta work!" his voice seemed to carry up the road in a gust of wind that smelt like bin bags and vomit.

"You'll pay. You will fucking pay!" I kept repeating... walking, walking quickly, and then finally running back to the Rowton.

I must have been wearing a scowl because no one spoke to me in the Rowton's lobby.

I pushed for the lift, but it took too long, so I went up the stairs.

My lungs felt like they were haemorrhaging by the time I reached my floor, my door and then collapsed into my room.

I fell onto the mattress and heaved deep breaths.

I was stone-cold sober now.

Scared.

And enraged.

After my breathing settled, I got the message up again and pressed to *call* the number it had been sent from.

It rang...

The bastards made me wait.

It felt like an eternity.

They knew what they were doing.

(And suddenly, they were torturing *two* people, not just the one.)

The call was finally accepted -

"Hello?" I asked.

"Patrick, hi," I recognised Theo Oak's voice in a heartbeat.

"You smug shitheel, you let him go right now."

"Patrick, calm down."

"Don't tell me to calm down you slag - you cunt!"

"Patrick, I'll hang up. I'll hang up and let the lads carry on with him for a few more minutes. Is that what you want?"

"I'm going to fucking kill you, Oak. Do you understand that?"

"No, you're not. You're going to calm down."

I found myself listening in silence. I was his bitch... already.

"We know you broke into John's house, Patrick. We know you cloned some files, stole some things. Some things we don't want seen. You understand?"

I couldn't bring myself to respond.

Oak continued –

"We want it all. We want it all and we want the DNA."

"You'll get nothing," I grunted.

"That's fine. If that's your position."

"But you have to let him go!"

"Wake up, Patrick. You're smart - smarter than I'd given you credit. If you don't play ball, then we'll gut this wanker and they'll never find any of him."

I didn't bother thinking.

*What was the point?*

I didn't have a choice.

"I understand," I said.

"That's what we wanted to hear."

"What do you want me to do?"

"You've been to John's house before. You know where it is. Bring everything we want to John's house, and then your friend will be released."

"How can I trust you?"

"You can't."

"So why should I do what you want?"

He sighed. "It's up to you. If you choose to trust us, then he has a chance. If you don't, then he has nothing."

"Okay."

"*Okay*, what?"

"I'll do it."

"Good boy."

The line went dead.

And in the quiet hotel room, I seethed...

## 42

The terraced house in Hall Green was not like any of the others. The others stood silent. And although the structures were identical, the activities within them were not.

During the night, voices had left its windows, as well as music and smells.

Cigarette smoke hung around the pavement outside like two pals chatting.

The occasional shout. A burst of laughter. The roar of a row. The skipping of a song. The jumping of music – louder and quieter.

For hours and hours. From midday, through the afternoon and evening, climaxing in the night-time, before slowly withering and dying in the early hours of the fresh day.

When the sun had finally clawed its way above the roofs opposite, pouring sunlight down upon it, the activities had all but ended. And then – all of a sudden – it was just like all the others...

A line of quiet structures.

Identical and morbid –

Just like headstones.

It was at that moment, that the first sign of life stepped foot from within. The first sign of life for many hours...

The man was in his twenties. He looked in good nick, considering the session he had been on. His clothes looked clean, but on closer inspection they were soaked with sweat, spilt beer and nicotine stench.

The man wiped his hair and staggered down the front drive to a tree by the road.

Then he undid his fly and let himself hang out.

He looked up and down, hoping for a motorist or a pedestrian to see him – but there was no one.

He looked at the windows in the houses that lined both sides of the road. He hoped for someone, anyone - an old lady, a young child - to see him, but again, there was no one.

He stared at himself for a moment, then he summoned up a thick, yellowy phlegm and spat it out into the road.

He stared at the spit.

Then he wiped his hair again, before finally putting himself away and lighting another cigarette.

He was swaying, but savvy enough to appear sober if he needed to.

The man lit a cigarette and started walking down Sarehole Road to where he'd parked.

His earlier exhibitionism had left him unfulfilled, so he took his phone out of his pocket and checked it. There were two unread messages.

During the night, while he'd been high, he'd sent pictures of himself in various stages of undress and arousal to two underaged girls. He'd been chatting with these girls for a fortnight or so. They both thought he was cool. He was older. He had a nice car. He took them to parties. He got them stoned and drunk and treated them like they were older and more important. He had worked them perfectly. Like he always did. He was good at it. That was his trade.

"I am the bollocks," he slurred to himself, throwing the half-finished cigarette up someone's drive and fiddling in his pocket for his car keys.

The white Range Rover was parked at a funny angle on the pavement.

It would have been obvious to any copper worth his salt that the bloke who parked it had been inebriated.

But the world remained the way it always did...

And cunts like him got by just fine.

Undeserved luck. He was dipped in it. Since birth, it seemed.

But that morning, on Sarehole Road in Hall Green, Theo Oak Jr's luck had just about run out...

# 43

I belted him across the back of the head with Putlog, and he dropped like a sack of shite.

*Not too hard, Hassle!* I'd told myself as I'd pulled back to swing.

I didn't want to kill the prick – just spark him.

He was moaning on the pavement, foaming at the mouth and jittering about like an epileptic. But that didn't concern me too much.

I half fancied pinching the Range, but I couldn't bring myself to even *steal* a white fucking Range Rover. I wasn't a rapper. And I wasn't pretending to be a millionaire. *So why would I want one?*

Instead, I dragged the vibrating nonce across to the Juara.

It had been parked behind, and the dickhead hadn't spotted it (or me).

I'd been waiting for hours outside the terrace after I'd got the scoop from Patrice as to where he was. I'd drank Holsten after Holsten, listening to album after album. (Most notably *Billy Lee Riley*, a rockabilly musician I had recently discovered. His covers of *Parchment Farm* and *St. James Infirmary* were particularly good.)

The nonce fitted perfectly in the boot. It was almost as though it had been designed with nonce-abduction in mind.

"Maybe?" I shrugged to myself, as I closed it.

Then I looked up and down the road.

Just like before, when he'd been hoping someone would see his dick - there was no one around.

"Piece of piss," I chuckled to myself, clambering into the Juara and starting the baby up.

*Was I going to play ball with Theo Oak?*

Was I fuck.

# 44

"SITTIN' DOWN HERE ON PARCHMENT FARM!" I sang along to Billy Ray as I drove.

I was legally drunk, bawling rockabilly and driving to Digbeth with a sex offender trapped inside my boot -

At that moment, I knew I hadn't lost it.

Life was as usual.

I could hear knocking from inside the boot and some screaming. Junior couldn't have known what hit him. One moment he was *the bollocks* and the next he was in complete darkness, hearing odd music and being thrown about by erratic driving.

I ignored him.

I drove from Sarehole Road and headed up Wake Green Road. Then I stopped outside The Covered Wagon pub. It was only seven in the morning, but I'd put a special order into the chef. He'd owed me a favour.

"Prawn Jalfrezi, Mushroom Rice," I'd said.

"Anything else?"

"Erm… Butter Chicken, probably. And a couple of naans."

(Butter Chicken was about the most perverted of the curry choices I could think. Junior would most likely appreciate it.)

I parked the car around the back of the pub, killed the engine, then walked over to the bin yard.

I banged four times on the door, and the chef opened up. He handed me the plastic bag. He nodded. I nodded back. And the favour had been done.

When I got back into the Juara, screaming had silenced.

I panicked for a moment that maybe he'd suffocated himself to death, either by accident, arousal or stupidity.

"Nah," I said, tearing off a bit of naan and washing it down with warm Holsten. "Can't be."

I started the car back up and headed Digbeth way.

The plan was unfolding itself step by step.

The end game was unknown to me at that moment.

But I was confident it would all work itself out.

As we tootled past St Mary's Row, down into Moseley, I glanced at The Elizabeth. Its doors were shut. The morning drinkers, last-night come-downers, down-and-outers, and the lay-abouters, were all milling around – lost. They reminded me of a rabble of funeral goers, awaiting the hearse. The Elizabeth was the last stop before sitting on a park bench, or in the square, clutching a can and ignoring the drizzle. They were all now at a crossroad and you could see it in their eyes...

I banged a right up the Alcester Road to take me back to the Rowton in Digbeth.

A bloke in a tweed suit and oiled moustache was walking some kind of extravagant terrier. He must have thought he was the dandy of Digbeth. But at some point, during his journey, he would have to bend over and pick up warm shit with his hand... Never forget that.

When I finally reached the hotel, I parked around the back, in a shady spot, were no eyes or ears were in distance.

I finished the last of the Holsten, fucked it into a laurel and opened the boot.

Junior was wide-eyed with terror, and he'd soiled himself. (A comedown in a car boot is never a good thing... trust me!)

"You make any noise and I'll bite your fucking eyes out, understand?"

He nodded.

His eyes adjusted to the light –

Then he seemed like he almost recognised me, just not where from.

"Get out," I pulled him out and the smell hit me hard. It wasn't good. And once again... the Juara had been soiled in.

I held a Stanley blade against his lower back. I told him that if he played up, I'd open his kidneys and let him bleed out in the bushes.

"Okay, man! Okay!" he whined.

The fire-exit to the stairwell was held open ajar by a brick – just as I'd left it.

We ascended the stairwell up to my floor.

Then we went down the corridor. (I held the Stanley extra tight at this point.)

Finally, we slipped into my room...

I let Junior go into the bathroom to clean himself up. He had a shower. I kept the door open, so he didn't lock himself inside or try any funny business.

When he was done, I gave him a change of clothes and handcuffed him to the radiator.

"Eat this, you scumbag," I said and threw the curry at him.

He sniffed it. "Butter Chicken!"

*Fucking knew it...*

He started eating it with one hand, but that made me feel sick, so I undid the cuffs until he finished.

I sat on the bed. The prawns were juicy and the rice was just divine. It was the first meal I'd had in days and my body was glad for it.

Then I cracked a can.

"So what are we doing here?" Junior asked.

"I've kidnapped you."

"Oh – right."

"Yes. I'd have thought that was obvious?"

"It was... yeah. I just..."

"You just thought you'd open your mouth for no reason?"

"Well, I -,"

"Just shut the fuck up."

He shut the fuck up.

I felt like explaining, even though I didn't have to –

"Your father has abducted a very close friend of mine. He's holding him ransom. He thinks I'm an idiot, you see? But I'm not, I'm -,"

"You're Paddy Hassle, right?"

I sighed. "How did you know?"

"I remember. You were on The Midnight Special, you fucked the whole party up, right?"

"That was me, yes."

"Dad said he's going to put your legs where your arms are."

"And I'll put your head where your arsehole is, if you don't shut up."

Junior shut up and started picking at a scrap of naan that lay discarded in his now cold curry.

I took it off him.

*Why had I bought a paedophile a curry anyway?*

I didn't know.

"Hold still," I told him, and took a picture of him chained to the radiator.

I looked at it –

"No, no, no. That's shite. You need to look scared."

"I am scared!"

"Well not enough!" I kicked him and he whimpered.

I snapped a picture quick –

"Ah, perfect..." I said when I looked at it.

I added a brief message to the picture. I wanted Apollo to be let free and for him to call me from The Elizabeth, then, and only then, would Junior be released from my capture.

After the message sent, I realised I'd have to wait.

My only company were a couple of tins of Holsten and a sex case.

"You're a private detective, right?" Junior spoke.

"I am."

"That's very interesting."

"It is."

There was a moment of silence.

"Jesus, this comedown is brutal," Junior sighed and shook his head.

"Well don't sniff cocaine then, dipshit."

"Nah, man. I had a few pipes."

"Pipes?"

"Crack. You ever tried it?"

I stood up, shook my head and walked across to the window.

I opened it an inch or so and lit a Chesterfield.

"Brilliant. A crackhead paedophile!"

"*Paedophile?*" I heard Junior squark like a crow.

"Keep it down!"

"I'm no paedophile, man."

"Oh no?"

"No, man. The girls come to me."

"So?"

"So, if they come to you then you're not a nonce."

"How'd you figure that?"

"I'm not going after them. I'm not *grooming them* or whatever. They want me. I just, indulge them, I suppose."

I shook my head. Theo Junior was more fucked-up than I thought. The evil bastard had convinced himself there was nothing wrong with him. And that was horrifying.

"Hey, Paddy, hey…" I heard the cuffs rattle as he leant towards me. "Let's do it, man."

"Do what?"

"Leave here. Let's get a couple of birds, a couple of pipes. We'll have a ball, man! Trust me, I can show you a good time."

I laughed.

"What d'you say?" he asked again.

"Just keep it down."

Talking to him made me need a piss.

When I was finished, I walked back into the room and checked my phone. There was still no response from Oak, but I could see that he had seen my message.

My heartbeat started to increase…

*What would his response be?*

"Hey, Paddy…"

"I swear to god, kid. If you don't keep quiet, I'll cut your tongue out!" I showed him the Stanley again.

"Where'd you get that jacket?" he asked anyway.

He was talking about my leather.

"It was my father's."

"Oh yeah?"

"Yes. It's genuine nineteen fifties. Not that that would mean jack shit, to a crackhead pervert like yourself."

"It's nice, man, real nice."

I gritted my teeth. "I-fucking-know-it-is."

"Man…" he trailed off. "If you should… you know… *die*… could I have it?"

I opened another tin of Holsten and lay down on the bed. The familiar stains and peels on the ceiling looked back to greet me.

"Yeah, sure. Why not…"

Some time passed. How long, I couldn't tell. Motors hummed outside, people walked past my door, but Junior didn't make a sound. He was too fucking stupid to try and escape. (I suppose he was smart enough to know that.)

"Paddy?" he finally broke the silence.

"What?"

"If you let me go, I won't do anything with anymore girls, man."

I kept quiet.

"I'll change, Paddy. I'll change, I promise…"

I thought about Junior. I thought about the old man. I thought about my family. Then I spoke:

"People never change. They just get better at hiding who they really are."

Whether he didn't understand what I'd said – or wasn't smart enough to respond – he didn't say another word.

And in that second lapse of total silence, my phone began to ring.

I picked it up to look at it -

It was John Stod.

# 45

"Long time no speak," I said.

"Indeed, Mr Hassle."

Fuck! His voice hadn't changed at all. He was still the prepubescent boy with hay fever. He was still the prick.

"Well come on then, Stoddy boy. This isn't a gay sex line. I don't charge by the hour. What the hell do you want?"

(I heard Junior laugh.)

"The boy," he said.

"*A boy?*"

"What? No!"

"I knew it! I had you sussed from day dot, you -,"

"MR HASSLE, PLEASE!"

His pathetic attempt at shouting reminded me of our first ever meeting. Jesus, I should have just ignored the buzzing before I let him on up to my office.

"You are to release Theo Oak's son, Mr Hassle."

"And why would I do that, shithead?"

"It is in your interest."

"No, it isn't. It's the opposite of my interest. He's my only leverage. Releasing him would be the complete opposite of *in my interest*."

"Mr Hassle, it is in your interest."

"Stop saying that."

"Well then, sir. You leave me no choice..."

"ooooooooh!" I howled. "What're you going to do, darling?"

"You will see."

The phone went dead.

I hadn't missed him.

He drained me. Every word. Every conversation. Just painful.

"You know Stod, right?" I asked Junior.

"Yes."

"Well, I think he just tried to threaten me. But I'm not sure."

Junior shrugged.

"He's a small fry," Junior carried on. "Dad's eating him up."

My ears picked up –

Here I had the son of Val Vulva's murderer –

He might know things –

And he was a complete invalid –

Easy to manipulate -

*Why hadn't you thought of this sooner, Hassle?*

"What do you mean, kid?" I asked him.

"It's what Dad does. He suckers people in, then milks them dry. Finds their weakness... cards, powder, women, whatever. Then he gets them in his pocket. Dad can offer all the vices you can think of. And over the next few years he bleeds them dry – sucks their marrow out, even."

"So what does Stod have?"

"Money. Connections in music. He's a producer, you know?"

"You don't say."

"John was in debt. His lady was spending quicker than he could earn. So, he went to his lady's boss to get bailed out – my Dad."

"Wait... so Oak owns Legs Thirteen?"

"He *owns* that part of town. Maybe not during the day – when the shops, the cops and the public are around. But when the sun sets, my Dad is the king."

It made sense now. Oak had spotted Stod coming a mile away, when he waltzed into Legs Thirteen and bought the love of a gorgeous stripper. Oak was ten steps ahead of him. And now he owned him...and The Gulldongs.

"Hang on a minute, have you ever heard of a band called The -,"

The phone ringing cut me off.

I looked at it -

It was John Stod again.

"Hold on a minute," I told Junior.

It was a video call.

I took a deep breath –

And accepted –

I saw Apollo. Two burly looking men were tussling with him, overpowering him. I could hear Apollo screaming and Stod was shouting over the melee:

"You see, Mr Hassle? Do you see what happens?"

"What are you doing?" I shouted back.

The background came into focus – they were in a launderette.

The two burly men pushed Apollo's head into a tumble drier. He was screaming, but they forced him further inside, further, then stuffed his feet in and shut the door.

Crumblemeat was one of these men. I recognised him.

"How long to dry this load out, Meat?" I could hear Stod giggling.

"I've got two quid on me," Crumblemeat laughed back, checking his pockets.

"That's twenty minutes, isn't it?"

"It sure is."

Crumblemeat put the two pounds into the machine and pressed on.

Inside the machine, I could see Apollo being tossed around and around, screaming as the heat increased and soldered his flesh.

"ENOUGH!" I shouted, jumping up off the bed. "ENOUGH!"

"What was that, Mr Hassle?" Stod asked.

"DONE! DONE! WHATEVER YOU WANT!"

"I can't hear you?"

The machine was still spinning -

Faster and faster -

Hotter and hotter -

"STOP IT!"

"Very well..." Stod sighed. "Meat?"

Crumblemeat opened the door and Apollo's body half slumped out, his skin was steaming, and he was panting loudly.

The video went shaky as the phone was passed hands –

Then Oak's face popped up on the screen.

"I half respect you, Patrick. You know that? You've got some bottle," he said.

I said nothing.

"Kidnapping my lad? No one in Birmingham would have dared. You know, in another life, I could have used you. I could have made you rich, got you anything you wanted. But you had to be a loser from Moseley..."

Again, I held my tongue.

"Well, you upped the stakes, prick. And then you lost. So you know what that means? It means you're done."

"Done?" I asked.

Theo Oak checked his Rolex. "You've got till noon."

"To do what?"

He grinned. "Kill yourself."

It didn't register what he'd said. "What?"

"You heard me – kill yourself. I want it public. I want you dead and named by noon today. I've got connections in West Midlands police, don't you worry. I'll know the identity of the body before the press does."

"So - wait, *you want me to kill myself?*"

"Yes. By noon. Let my son go and kill yourself. Kill yourself publicly."

"I..."

"Sorry, Patrick. Like I said, mate – you upped the stakes and then you lost, so the cost is much higher. We were playing a man's game, and this is the price. I'm sure you understand," he smirked at me.

I took a deep breath and hung my head. I waited for a moment before I spoke. "And Apollo?"

Oak nodded. "See, I told them you were a good bloke. Always concerned about your pal before yourself. Fuck it, yeah, I'll let him go. He's no good to me anyway."

"Your word?"

"Patrick, my friend. I don't do this often. But yeah, I give you my word."

I didn't have anything left to say.

For a second, I glanced across at Junior...

He was grinning at me. He'd heard the whole thing. And he'd heard how his Daddy, once again, had saved his worthless arse.

"Okay," I said.

"I knew I could count on you," Oak smiled. "Oh, and Patrick?"

"Yes?"

"I don't have to explain to you the implications of a suicide that doesn't happen, do I? Or a suicide that happens at *ten past twelve*?"

"What?"

"Well… we've got a bit of change left here, for another cycle…"

I heard sick laughter erupt on his side of the line, from the goons and from Stod.

"I understand."

"You've got an hour and a half. Tie up your loose ends, then get it done."

The line went dead.

I looked across at Junior –

And he was still grinning at me.

# 46

The walk to Moor Street Train Station was quick – too quick. I felt like stopping at The Anchor on the way and sinking a final pint, but for two reasons I didn't. One – so the memory of the place remained one of hope and happiness, not of impending demise. And two – because I felt like I had to look death in the eye and face her sober. No crutch. No Dutch Courage. Just plain me.

Junior tried to be nice to me. He was a psychopath – bereft of the feeling of pity. But no doubt, in his deranged mind, it made him feel great to jest around the emotion.

"I'm sorry, Paddy."

"It's okay. It had to happen someday."

"Do you want me to kill you?"

"Thanks, that's nice of you. But no."

"What're you going to do?"

"Jump under a train."

"A moving one?"

I looked at him.

"Yeah, that's probably quick," Junior said.

"Unless I miss."

"If you miss, I promise I'll club you to death or something."

"You would? For me?"

He couldn't tell I was joking.

(Man, I wanted to punch him in the throat as hard as I could.)

When we reached Moor Street, I lit a Chesterfield and just hung around by the gates for a bit. I smoked. I smoked. Time moved and moved. It waited for no one. It wasn't going to wait for Hassle.

*Was this it then?*

*Stod and Oak go free?*

*Val Vulva turns to ash without justice served?*

*The world remains corrupt?*

*The evil keep on going?*

*The good keep on dying?*

*And no one bats a fucking eyelid?*

"Yeah, probably," I threw a fag end away and a tramp picked it up immediately. "It's been that way since day one, why should it change for you?" I berated myself.

"Paddy, the train's almost here," I heard Junior say.

"What?"

"The next train to arrive."

"Dickhead, I'm not jumping under a train that's *arriving*."

"Why?"

"Because it's slowing down... it's fucking arriving."

"So how're you going to do it?"

"I'm going to ask him," I pointed at the man at the ticket office.

"Ask him what?"

"When the next train is passing through."

"Won't that be suspicious?"

"Oh fucking hell, let me do the thinking, Junior!"

Maybe death wouldn't be that bad. At its worst, what would it be? Black. Empty. Nothing. Like that gap between dreams and awaking. You don't dream for the full eight hours, do you? There are minutes, hours, hours and hours, when you're just in the darkness. If that was the worst it could be - darkness - then the worst wasn't that bad.

Then glue-heads started bugging me.

They had plastic bags full of Evo-Stik up their sleeves and heaved deep breaths from them every few moments. Then they wandered over to me and started asking for things. One of them asked if he could comb my hair.

"Typical," I said. Even at my end, it was the scum that forced me to do it.

I strutted over to the ticket man.

I wanted to die confident.

"Hello," I said.

"Yes, sir?"

"When's the next train passing through?"

"*Passing through?*"

"Yeah, you know, like *not stopping.*"

He paused. He was wearing sunglasses. He was in his mid-twenties and must have thought he looked cool. I wanted to take them off and crush them in my hand. I wanted to tell him to take them off and face reality. Be a man, not an American.

"Why would you want to know that?" he asked.

"Well, Columbo, I'm a train enthusiast. I want to watch."

"In that case, sir, let me check."

He fucked about on a computer for a bit.

"Ah, yes," he said.

"So when is it?"

"Lucky for you, sir, it's in ten minutes."

"Yeah... lucky. Well thanks."

"Excuse me, sir. The barriers are in use. You will have to pay."

"What?"

"I'll have to charge you."

"What – to watch a fucking train? I'm not getting on it."

"Sir, the barriers are down."

"And? I can hop them."

"You certainly cannot!"

"Are you actually charging me to look at a train go past?"

"Those are the rules."

I sighed.

I had to pay to die.

The bastard was charging me to end my life…

Maybe the communists were right. Had I battled against the Bolsheviks in Moseley for no reason? They were right! Damn it, they were right!

I considered telling him I was going to jump, but National Rail probably had a suicide charge: *Blow yourself to bits! No problem. But don't expect us to hose the tracks for free!*

"How much then?" I snarled.

"That'll be…" he fucked about again. "Seventy-five pence."

"Here's a quid, have a nice day."

I walked over to the barriers with my ticket, and I could have sworn the plastic arms were laughing as they raised and let me and Junior through.

We went and stood on the platform. It was fairly quiet. The only people were minding their own business – listening to music, reading the paper or staring at their shoes.

Junior tried to make small talk, but I wasn't listening.

My mind was on death. No more wondering, fearing or fantasising. Soon it would be my reality – my only reality.

I decided the worst death was not darkness –

It was heaven.

A heaven full of family members.

And family members full of disappointment and scorn.

"Jesus, spare me from that!" I begged.

"What's that, Paddy?" Junior asked.

"Nothing. That shade-wearing bellend at the ticket office has pissed me off!"

"That's not nice, he was blind!" moralised the paedophile.

"He wasn't blind."

"Yes, he was. The keyboard was brail. And he had a guide dog under the desk. Didn't you see?"

"Of course I did."

"So what do you -,"

"Shut up!" I barked.

After a few moments, I took my father's old jacket off. It was my favourite possession. But I wouldn't be needing it where I was going.

"Here you go," I passed it over to Junior.

"Really?"

"Yeah."

"Your wallet's in here," he said.

"And some fags. I won't need either."

The train was beginning to rumble closer from the distance.

I wondered what song they'd play at my funeral.

And then I didn't care.

*Fuck the funeral! What song was I going to go out to?*

There were so many choices, I didn't know what to pick.

*Danny Boy?*

I almost asked Junior to sing it for me, then I realised that would have been ridiculous – serenaded into the afterlife by a crack-head nonce.

I turned my back to the silhouette of the train on the horizon. I couldn't bring myself to watch it rise and begin towards me…

It was getting louder and louder - nearer and nearer.

The platform was trembling.

I needed to distract myself.

"What're you going to do today, Junior?" I asked.

My mouth was dry and my knees were trembling.

"Oh, I don't know…" he started thinking.

I could hear the train ringing.

It was pulling in.

It was close.

Death was waiting. I could smell her. Pinewood and gin.

"I think I'll get smashed," Junior grinned, and I noticed he was holding his phone towards me – recording it all.

Then I looked up to see my father watching from the end of the platform. He was laughing.

"You're right about that," I said to Junior.

A horn sounded – the time was now!

"What d'you mean?" he asked -

And I threw him under it.

# 47

I'd killed the kid. The last flash of an image I'd seen, was meat peeling from bone, disappearing under the metal. He never knew what hit him. But I did. And that image would be with me forever. It was *something else* I'd have to deal with – but not at that moment – I didn't have time.

The police would think it was me who was mangled between the tracks at Moor Street Train Station.

They'd find my ID in the wallet.

That bought me some time.

Of course, they'd do more tests and find the ripped-up corpse was really that of Theo Oak Jr.

But it bought me time...

Time to save Apollo.

And time to get the drop on Oak and Stod.

After the kid disappeared in a flash of red and black, I'd turned on my heels and walked quickly up the stairs. (Never run!) I walked quickly up them, over the platforms and then out past the blind ticket man.

The screams were delayed.

People had disbelieved their eyes.

And by then, I was already amongst glue-heads, making my escape.

I handed one of them a fiver. "It's good to be alive, isn't it?"

"Urrrwwaaa," he agreed.

My body felt like it was on an amphetamine rush, paired with that two-drink giddiness.

Half an hour ago, on the walk to the station, while I was taking my last mile, Mrs Stod had messaged me.

(I hadn't let Junior see.)

She said she needed to meet with me. She had proof that John

Stod and Theo Oak were planning on murdering Val Vulva. I hadn't had time to second guess her. That was the leverage I needed. And she described the evidence as *undeniable*. That word kept bouncing around in my head, echoing – *undeniable*.

Back at the Rowton, I packed my road-kit quickly.

I said goodbye to the room, settled-up at the desk and clambered into the Juara which was still parked behind the hotel.

I needed to head back to Moseley – back to where it all started.

I needed to make sure Apollo was okay.

I needed to get this evidence from Mrs Stod.

And then I could have my revenge.

# 48

The flat cap was low and Chesterfield lit. I felt like Hassle again, creaking in the shadows on the Moseley square. The benches were empty, and this was strange. The benches were always home to someone – heroin addicts sleeping, drunkards still yelling or nutters still raving. It may as well have been a funeral parlour after closing. Only the wind, the leaves and Hassle were standing on the pavement at that time.

The night was bringing something with it –

And I was coming up on whatever it was –

Doom.

It was just before midnight, and it must have been a weekday – because all of Moseley was quiet, when a white Mercedes Sprinter van rumbled down Wake Green Road. It banged a left, and then another left, driving up the entry by the shop and my flat, descending into the carpark at the back of The Elizabeth.

I threw the fag end down the road and crossed.

I passed up a narrow entry and could hear the rumbling of the Sprinter's engine just ahead of me.

Then suddenly it roared –

A gear shifted –

I darted from the entry into the carpark –

But it was gone.

I lit another cigarette and jogged over to The Elizabeth's back doors. They were unlocked. A light was on inside. And I saw Apollo, dragging himself across to the bar.

*Theo Oak had kept his word...*

"Apollo!" I opened the door and rushed over to him.

He was weak. His hair was matted and clumpy from all his blood, now dried. And his face was purple with swelling.

"They done me over good, brother," he coughed.

I sat him down. Then I locked the back door.

"I'll fix you a rum," I said.

"I don't want one."

"I'll fix you a double."

I put a double Cracken in a tumbler neat and slid it across to him. Then I wrapped a fistful of ice in a dishtowel, knotted it up and pressed it against his head.

"Those bastards. Don't you worry, Apollo. They'll pay."

"Hassle…"

"I'll sort them for you. Those dirty, scheming, fucking bastards!"

"Hassle!"

Apollo was glaring at me. He'd refused the rum.

"What's wrong?" I asked.

"Leave."

"*Leave it?* I'm not leaving it. They nearly killed my friend. They're going to pay, with teeth and bones, they'll fucking pay!"

"No – LEAVE!"

"*Leave?*"

"Hass, they think you're dead. Get out of here. Leave! Quick!"

I shook my head.

"You hear me?" Apollo grabbed my neck. Even in his weakened state, his giant fist contracted with the strength of a Boa. "You dumb fucker… I SAID LEAVE!"

I wrestled loose. "I'm not going anywhere."

Apollo hit the rum – dry. "They'll kill you. No two ways about it. No ifs. No buts. They'll kill you."

"Oh, we'll see about -,"

"Fucking hell, Hassle! This isn't time for dick measuring, bro!"

"I'm not measuring jack! This is principal."

"This is life and death!"

I slammed my fist onto the bar. "Wake up, man! What life do I have other than this place? Moseley, you, the bums, the cases, the

199

aggro. Here I'm Hassle. Here I've got a purpose. Where can I go? What can I do? I'd rather die here with purpose, than live on as fuck-all!"

He must have seen the sincerity in my eyes because he kept quiet.

"I've got to get you sorted out," I pulled him up.

"I'm fine."

"You're all over the place. Is the first aid kit upstairs, in the office?"

"Yeah."

"Come on then."

"Bring the bottle."

I snatched up the Cracken and helped him up the stairs.

The windows all around the pub were perfect sheets of darkness –

Eyes could have been looking in from every one of them –

Eyes of who knows?...

Looking at two ghosts, deciding on how to kill them for good.

# 49

I called the chick Ronda.

Apollo had collapsed at the top of the stairs, and I didn't know how to help him. She arrived in five minutes – calm, collected and totally in control. The complete opposite of everything I was.

"Hello, *John Butler*..." she smiled.

"Okay, cut it. You know I'm Paddy Hassle."

She had Apollo lying down on a fold-out bed. He'd hit the Cracken pretty hard and had passed out. She'd woken him up to give him some painkillers, then cleaned his wounds and cooled his swelling. She was the kind of squeeze I needed in my life.

"Is he going to be okay?" I asked.

(I hit the Cracken too.)

"He'll be okay. He's been in states like this before, you know?"

"I know."

"He'll be banged up for a few weeks, but nothing permanent."

"You a nurse?"

"No. My friends are all drinkers."

"That's better than a nurse."

Ronda laughed. "You're not a bad guy, Hassle. You're a good friend to Apollo."

"He's my only bloody friend."

"You're nothing like what people say about you."

I stood up and lit a Chesterfield. "What do they say?"

"Oh that you're mean, drunk, ignorant... *racist*."

"Racist?"

She nodded. "I've heard that a couple of times."

"How can I be racist? All my dealers are black."

Ronda laughed and I laughed too.

"You see that kind of thing could get taken very wrongly in Moseley!" she waved a finger.

"Don't I know it."

I walked across to the window and opened it.

The night air was refreshing.

I finished my cigarette and messaged Mrs Stod.

I needed to meet with her soon.

I needed the evidence before Junior was identified as the real suicide. That would be the catalyst for a lot of body dropping – me, Apollo, maybe even Mrs Stod...Ronda...anyone who was close.

"What's going on, Paddy?" I heard Ronda ask behind me.

I finished texting. "Just something got out of hand."

"Out of hand? They could have killed Apollo!"

"Trust me, it's nothing."

"Really?" she didn't believe me.

"Well – maybe it's more than nothing. But I can handle it."

"No, you can't."

I heard her stand up. She walked up behind me and put a hand on my shoulder. "You're a strong man. But your strength makes you weak."

I span around. "And you're too smart for your own good, kid!" I gently tapped a clenched fist against her chin, then I sat down by Apollo and hit the Cracken a couple more times.

"Hass..." I heard Apollo moan from his sleep.

"Yes, my friend," I took his hand and squeezed it.

"Please..."

"Please what?"

"Don't do..."

"What?"

"Don't do...anything stupid..."

"Would I?" I smirked, then I kissed his hand and laid it down.

The man had taken beatings, torture, pain and threats beyond my conception – and he had done it all because of me. I owed him my life as a minimum. That was obvious.

"Hass…"

"Apollo, rest!" I commanded and patted his head.

"I don't get it…" he slurred.

"Don't get what, pal?"

"They thought you were dead…"

I heard Ronda walk closer – interested.

"I was."

"But you had his kid, didn't you?"

Even half-out-of-it, he was sharp. "Yeah, I had his kid."

"They said you'd killed yourself… They said you'd jumped in front of a train…"

I said nothing.

Then Apollo sat up. His eyes rolled over, back to life -

"It was the kid! You killed his kid, didn't you?"

Again, I said nothing. I just lowered him back to the bed by his shoulders.

"Rest," I told him again, and then I stood up.

The chick Ronda was looking at me. She was looking at me in a way she hadn't before. She said nothing and walked across to a chair in the corner. Then she sat down and stared at the wall ahead of her.

She'd thought I was a good man.

She'd thought strength had made me weak.

Well, kindness had made her stupid.

I wasn't a good man.

I was a thief, a charlatan, a murderer – and I'd slipped right past her defences. She was a strong woman, a smart woman. But at that moment in the dingy room above The Elizabeth – she was re-evaluating her whole morality…

Apollo sat up again suddenly, and it made us both jump.

"Apollo, darling!" Ronda rushed past me to get to him.

"What's wrong?" I stood up.

"Are you both deaf?" he grunted, swinging his legs from the bed.

"What?" we both asked.

"Someone's knocking outside!"

Ronda and I were both so zoned that we hadn't heard.

"I'll get it," I said.

"Fucking hell!" Apollo pulled away from both of us. "I'm not a fucking child. I can walk!"

He hobbled across to the door. When he passed through it, he left it open, and I heard him limping down the stairs.

Ronda looked at me, but when my eyes met hers, she averted them quickly.

"BLOOD AND FIRE!" Apollo shouted from below.

I darted out the door and down the stairs.

Apollo turned and looked at me - his mouth was wide with shock.

He stepped aside from the open front door, and Mrs Stod walked in...


Her face had been battered into a pulp.

# 50

"What the hell happened to you?" I took her and led her upstairs.

"Please, Paddy. It's nothing..."

"Get upstairs."

Ronda took her by the hand and led her the rest of the way. I helped Apollo back up, but not before locking and double checking all the doors.

There was fear tremoring inside me –

Any moment, any second, I felt something could happen –

We were all in danger.

"Again – what the fuck happened to you?" I asked when I was back up with the rest of them.

"Paddy, she needs some -," Ronda protested, so I pushed her aside.

"PADDY!" I heard Apollo shout.

"Damn it, I won't ask you again?" I grabbed Mrs Stod's wrist and felt my jaw muscles tighten. "Who did this to you?"

She started crying.

"Talk!" I shouted.

"John did it..." she whimpered and hung her head low.

She was a mess.

He'd given her a few right hooks.

Her right eye was swollen shut, her jawline was swollen on the right side and a dark, blue bruise was rising on her right cheek. The little bastard couldn't even string a combination together, he had to swing and swing with his wanking arm. But at least I knew which one to break.

"Why'd he do it? Did he find out?"

"Apollo, let's leave," Ronda helped him up and took him into another upstairs room.

"No. He was drunk," she explained to me.

"AND?"

"And he's broke. He's lost everything!"

"So?"

"So, he took it out on me!"

I took a few deep breaths. "Have you got it?"

"Got what?" she mumbled.

I knelt beside her. "The proof I need."

"I've got a recording."

"Of what?"

"John and Oak talking."

"You recorded them?"

"His office is bugged."

"Stod's?"

"Yes. I bugged it a while back when he started accusing me. I thought things might get worse."

"You cold bitch," I smiled.

"I had to. I had to have something to use against him. No way, Paddy... No way am I going back to those estates and that bullshit! That piece of shit has had years of my life. The things I had to do for him... to please him... He owes me! He owes me a living! I'll get what I deserve!"

She was ferocious.

Even when bruised and battered, she was a wild animal.

But I needed to keep on track. I needed to remember where I was in this whole thing.

"What does the recording say?" I asked.

"...everything that you need..." she smiled through the swelling.

"Don't lead me on, baby!"

"The murder. They're talking about it."

"You got it?"

"Yeah."

"Show me."

She took her phone out of her jean pocket. She fumbled for a second, loading up a voice clip, then pressed play...

It was beautiful.

Music to my ears.

Stod and Oak, discussing the problems with Val Vulva – his unpredictability, unprofessionalism, the drug and alcohol problems and the negative press he would attract The Gulldongs.

And then – plotting his murder...

Stod gave Oak the hotel room number at the Radison and a key to it that he had acquired.

Oak mentioned Crumblemeat – his deadliest buttonman – and guaranteed the deed would be done.

This was it. I had it. Finally! Proof. Undeniable proof. I was free!

Not only that, but we were all together. Safe. At least for the time being – safely locked inside a pub. I'd call the police, get CID around, and hand over all the evidence I had – the documents I cloned from Stod's, the voice recording of their plotting and DNA evidence from Crumblemeat the murderer. This was it. *Paddy Hassle, had won again!* We could all drink and celebrate while we waited for the blue lights to arrive.

I leant over and kissed Mrs Stod on the cheek –

She flinched from the pain.

And then, suddenly, my freedom disappeared again – disappeared to nothing...

I wasn't free. I wasn't free at all.

I still had debts unpaid.

I had a debt to Apollo. And I had a debt to the bird.

So, I asked her:

"Is Stod in?"

# 51

They all begged me not to go. But I didn't listen.

Duty was sacred. Wellbeing was meaningless. That was how I looked at it. And debt was a duty. I couldn't bring myself to scurry away, like some rodent, a creature only concerned with its own welfare - to hand over the evidence and then wait, safe and locked inside a pub. *How pathetic!* Stod and Oak had crossed a line. They had to pay. And at *my* hands.

Don't be confused –

I wasn't doing this for Apollo or for Mrs Stod –

I was doing this for myself, and my own selfish reasons.

Before I'd left, I handed over all the evidence to them.

I explained the saga in depth. Apollo, Ronda and Mrs Stod were all very clear on what had happened. From my first meeting with Stod, through to finding Val Vulva, through to where we all were now - and everything in between.

Ronda called the police and explained the situation. The coppers told us to remain where we were - someone was coming immediately.

"Paddy, please!" Ronda had said as I pulled my flat cap on.

"Just look after them," I told her, then I left.

The rain had started in Moseley.

It had been waiting for me while I was inside - then let loose as soon as I stepped foot on the pavement.

I walked around the corner and paused outside the shop below my flat. I did some stretches:

First the lower back. Then the hips. Shoulders. Wrists and knees.

Nearby pedestrians gave me a wide birth, but by my warm-up's completion I was supple - ready for a skirmish.

The old man who owned the shop stepped outside to smoke one of his revolting Indian cigarettes.

"What are you doing?" he asked.

"I'm off to kill a man."

"Good luck, sir!" he boomed with the confidence of the Raj, then headed back inside the shop with his cigarette still lit. (I wasn't sure if he hadn't understood, or just didn't give a fuck.)

Carrying on up the Alcester Road in the rain, I thought back to what had led me to where I was –

I couldn't help but think about her.

And in turn, I couldn't help but think about him.

Just like outside The Anchor, a wind picked up – and brought his scent up the road. He was always around. Ever present. Ubiquitous! He was a leaking gutter. He was a flooded drain. He was fly-tipped rubbish amongst nettles. He was every bit of filth that blemished pavements, stained bus seats, and subsided old brickwork walls. He was every impurity in the world, and every impurity in me. And his breath was unmistakeable – a cold burning, cold like death with a caustic burn of liquor. (I felt it begin on the back of my neck...)

"I don't need you," I said, listening to his footsteps behind me.

"You know everthin, don't ye, boy?"

"What do you want?"

"Just tae watch. Tae see if ye've the bottle, dis time."

"I've got bottle."

"HA!" he coughed like a Diesel engine. "Neevah saw it meself!"

"I was going to. I was -,"

"But ye didn't... *did ye?*"

His final two words were close. Painfully close. My ears twitched.

"LEAVE ME ALONE!" I span around swinging and scratching, kicking and spitting – but the vacant night-time was all that my blows connected with.

He was gone again.

He was gone, but he was right.

He was right about me, and my cowardice, from all those years ago, and from one time in particular -

I'd revealed the story to Mrs Stod (one night after too many shorts back at the flat). She was the first person I'd ever recounted it to. And it was about the first time I'd ever tried to stand up to him...

I was fifteen years old.

I'd just got home from school, and I knew that *it* had happened again. How? Because the kitchen door was shut, and the living room was empty.

My mother never shut the kitchen door. It was always open, carrying smells of dinner and songs from her music collection – *Revolver, Beggar's Banquet, Turn! Turn! Turn!* - she introduced me to all the greats.

The kitchen door was only ever shut if she was hiding something. And if the living room was empty, it meant he'd stormed off to the pub.

At that moment, home from school, I knew that barbarism had been done only moments ago.

I was nervous but I walked through the oddly silent living room anyway and opened the kitchen door.

He'd done a real number on her. The worst I'd ever seen.

My mother was cutting scallions and peeling potatoes when I walked in.

And then the usual –

"Oh, hello, my darling," she said without turning to face me.

She was ashamed. (In her mind, it was always her fault.)

*Oh, I should have just kept me quiet!* She'd always fucking say.

"Where is he?" I asked.

"He's out. Just out..."

Something inside me broke that afternoon. Something that had been strained, abused and battered for so long:

*Did deciding to kill him make me a strong child? Or instead, was it my first day as a weak man?*

Either way, as ham hock boiled and my mother bled, the decision to murder my father set like concrete in my mind.

I'd led her up the stairs to bed, then fetched Mrs O'Toole to tend to her wounds.

Against both their pleadings, I left for reasons of death.

I'd taken a carving knife from the kitchen draw and hidden it under my school blazer. I wasn't nervous and I wasn't scared at all. I was convinced I would do it. I had no doubt or hesitation, and it felt like the first good deed I'd ever done in my life.

I ran quickly to his local pub...

But I was one battering too late.

"That's his boy!" some slurring old paddy pointed at me.

My old man was being carried out on a stretcher.

"What's wrong with him?" I'd asked, holding the knife's handle under my blazer, and watching the paramedics take him away.

"He'll be fine, boy!" the old paddy said.

But his liver had finally given out -

Advanced cirrhosis.

He never left the hospital.

He never so much as got out of bed again.

But I visited him every day. And on every visit, I brought the carving knife with me.

I'd sit on the chair beside the bed and will him to get better. I wanted him to recover, just so I could kill him myself. I was certain that plunging the knife into him, over and over again, would make me feel better. It would make me feel better about the past, about who I was, what had happened and what still lay in store for me.

But the old bastard wouldn't give me the satisfaction.

During those couple of weeks, it was the only time I ever prayed. When my mother's swelling had gone down (at least enough to cover with makeup) she was at St Anne's every day – lighting candles, praying - and I was with her! I prayed for his recovery too!

"Am I a coward?" I'd ask myself on every visit to the hospital at his bedside, gripping the knife's handle and watching his chest rise and deflate with each undeserved breath.

*Was it goodness or cowardice that stopped me doing it?*

I could never tell.

But the nurses told me on every visit what a *lovely boy* I was to stay with my father. And when I arrived one day, to be told he'd died, they thought my tears and wailing were out of mourning.

Well, I suppose I was mourning... I was mourning myself! Any chance I'd had at redemption had breathed its last, merely an hour before I'd arrived. I was doomed to live the rest of my life as a victim. Never able to avenge myself. Never able to right the wrongs done against me. Never to be a hero... forever to be a pathetic victim.

That was what I was, for a long time, until fifteen-something years later, when the universe offered me a second chance:

Mrs Stod, looking like my mother, with a drunken wife beater's fist marks all over her face.

She was my bleeding, redeeming angel.

And I would not mess it up again.

"NOT AGAIN!" I assured myself.

I was on Reddings Road -

And John Stod's house was nearby.

## 52

Underneath a tree, I watched his house. The Daimler was still on the drive and the lights were on. He was in.

I had to do it. I was sure of that. But nonetheless a sober revolt in my brain told me I was being stupid. *You've got the evidence! What are you doing? All that hard work for nothing?* But I crushed the uprising with no mercy, Freikorp-style.

This was my last chance to get them – Stod and Oak. As soon as the police were involved, they'd both be whisked away into custody, remanded in jail, prosecuted in court and taken to prison.

And their prison-time would not be one of suffering either. I'd heard the stories – about what bird had turned into. Sex cases were kept in segregation, to stop the castrations. Women beaters and rapists were given *therapy.* Graduates, with circular glasses and small hands who cycled to work actually *pitied* these pieces of scum. They had televisions and biscuits in their cells. *Biscuits for paedophiles!* Drunken thugs could kick someone to death on a night out, plead guilty, have the charges reduced to manslaughter, and get ten years! They'd serve half on good behaviour.

No way. Not on my watch! My mind was made up.

But before I went in, I decided to call The Gulldongs:

"Hey, Hassle, what's poppin'?" Hopper answered.

"I got some news for you kids."

"What's that?"

"It was Stod and Oak."

"What?"

"They killed your friend. They killed Val Vulva."

Silence for a second. "Wait…what do you mean?"

"It's all there, Hopper. I've got all the evidence. It'll all be made clear to you. But I've got to go now."

"Hassle, wait! What's going on?"

"I'm dealing out the justice myself. Don't worry. They'll get it. We can't rely on the legal system of today!"

"Hassle, dude, what are you going to do, man?"

"I'm outside Stod's place now."

"Please, dude, explain what's going on!"

"Just know one thing - they're guilty. I've got all the evidence. Some colleagues of mine are holding onto it now, awaiting police protection at The Elizabeth of York."

"So why aren't you with them?"

"Because I can't be," I hung the phone up and started walking across the road.

An old book, one that had done my mother no good, once said *an eye for an eye*. (It rabbited on some other shite later on about *turning the other cheek*, but we'll ignore that for now.) The message I took from it, and from all my life, was to never turn the other cheek, never just accept, never just suffer alone and in silence. Stand up. An eye for an eye!

"And I'm going to pull John Stod's out of his fucking head!"

I hopped his gate and headed for the utility door.

I just knew it would be open.

The gods were on my side...

# 53

I found him in the kitchen. His eyes were red from tears and a bottle of Teachers whisky was half-empty on the table in front of him. John Stod, the-man-who-looked-like-a-leaking-bag-of-dog-shit, resembled every woman abuser in history.

"Mr Hassle?"

He didn't seem scared by my intrusion.

"I'm here to put you out of the game, Stod!"

"Very well," he hit the Teachers and wiped his greasy gob. "I'd welcome it."

I started for him across the kitchen floor –

"In fact, Mr Hassle, I would more than welcome it. If flocks of angels regaled my -,"

I grabbed him around the throat and got to work –

I pulled him up and Judo-tossed him onto the ground, then I locked my hands around his windpipe and started –

The trick was *not* to squeeze. (Squeezing is a beginner's mistake, one made by all amateur stranglers.) Instead, you lock your hands around their throat *lean on them*. Just like Bill Withers explained in his song. With all your weight and with all your hate.

I watched his eyes bulge and start to go dead. I imagined they were my fathers. I wanted to watch their pilot light go out.

But then I noticed something –

He wasn't putting up a fight.

His arms were laying limp by his sides –

He was letting me kill him!

"Fight back, you ponce!" I growled at him, through saliva and gritted teeth.

Reluctantly, I stopped.

He retched and coughed on the floor, regaining his breath, as life crept back inside him again. I'd taken him all the way to the edge and then I'd brought him back. (Maybe that was worse than death, if death was what he'd really wanted?)

"You'd let me kill you, wouldn't you?" I asked.

"There's nothing for me anymore!" he started to cry.

I got up and walked across to the kitchen island. I tried to think. I tried to decide what to do. But my mind was scattered.

I glanced outside into the dark garden. I could have sworn my father was grinning at me from the far end. Grinning, as if to say: *Ney bottle...*

"ENOUGH!"

I pulled a carving knife out of a block on the island and turned.

Stod was still on the floor, snivelling and shaking.

"I've got to do it, Stod!"

He thought for a moment. "Very well..."

I stormed across to him. "You just had to hurt her, didn't you?"

"What?"

"Did it make you feel better? Beating on a dame!"

"I never touched her!" he protested. "She left me!"

I got him standing and lined the knife up with his liver. It'd be slow. He'd be able to watch the life pump out and form a nice puddle around him.

"I loved her... I loved her..." he wept.

"You were supposed to protect her!" I gnarled. "She was your wife!" I pulled the blade back – ready to drive it in. "And he was your son! He was your son!"

"HOLD IT!" A voice shouted and a handgun cocked.

I snapped back to reality and turned -

Theo Oak was stood in the doorway to the hall, and Crumblemeat was beside him. Oak was aiming a Luger right at me.

"You can wait your turn," I told him.

Oak's face was pale with confusion. "You..."

He'd thought I was brown bread.

"Yeah, shitheel - ME!" I flashed a glib grin, and he said nothing. "Didn't I tell you I'd wipe that smile of your face?"

"Where is my son?" he finally asked.

"That's a hard question to answer, Theo... he's probably somewhere between Moor Street and Snow Hill."

It clicked –

"You killed him?"

"Yeah, just like all the poor fuckers you've clipped in the past."

"YOU KILLED HIM!"

Oak fired a shot –

Stod's innermost thoughts splattered up the side of my face. His body went dead, and we fell to the floor. Suddenly I was trapped underneath the prepubescent boy with hay fever.

Oak fired again –

I rolled Stod over, letting his cadaver take the damage for me.

*(Who'd have thought it? John Stod – finally coming in useful!)*

"I'LL KILL YOU! I'LL KILL YOU!" I could hear Oak shout.

Another shot.

Then a hollow click –

The Luger had jammed!

I rolled the body away and was up, carving knife in hand –

Oak reloaded –

"TAE FUCK WITH YA!" I thrusted the blade in his direction –

He put a round into my gut –

I sunk the blade into his shoulder and the pair of us went down to the ground.

Oak was on top –

But he'd dropped the shooter –

He was trying to wrestle the blade out of my hand –

"Meat…" Oak hissed like a viper. "He's mine!"

And in my peripherals, I saw the giant figure take a step back to watch us in our life-and-death struggle.

Oak had his fingers in my eyes – pushing hard.

But his thumb slipped into my mouth – so I bit down.

He was pulling the blade out of his shoulder –

And I was trying to force it in further –

"You dirty bastard! I'll kill you!" he groaned, managing to get the upper hand.

I felt the blade creeping out of his flesh –

If he got control of it, then I'd be as good as dead.

With my free hand I reached up and started fish-hooking him. (I had my thumb hooked inside his gob and started pulling his cheek sidewards, ripping it.)

"AAAARRRRRRGGHH!" he started yowling in pain.

I pulled hard –

The knife started sinking back in –

I was winning!

All those pissed-up nights in town, rolling around in a gutter with some other loser, they weren't for nothing!

"MEEEEEAT!" Oak screamed. "GET HIM!"

And then I was fucked.

I felt myself get hauled up off the floor –

Suddenly I was eight-foot in the air, admiring Stod's watermark-free ceiling.

"Kill him for fuck's sake!" Oak moaned from below.

Then out of nowhere –

THWACK!!! –

The sound of wood smashing into a million pieces –

I fell through the air and landed hard on the ground –

I turned quickly –

*What had happened? –*

The Gulldongs…

Crumblemeat was unconscious on the floor and Patrice was stood behind him, holding all that was left of the neck of a bass.

Hopper rushed in too, with a mic stand and Scratch Man was holding two drumsticks like they were Ninja daggers.

The Gulldongs had saved me.

"Hassle, are you okay?" Hopper rushed over and helped me up.

"Oak plugged me. But I'll live."

I glanced at my would-be murderer – the big, bad Theo Oak was like a pathetic child – submissive and weeping on the floor. He'd been beat, and he knew it.

"We've got to get you to a hospital," Hopper said to me.

"That sounds like a good idea…" I slurred.

They sat me back down again and I felt darkness – old familiar darkness – begin to creep all around and sing me a gentle lullaby to sleep…

## 54

I was in the QE Hospital for just under a week. Surgery had removed the bullet from my gut, and I'd slept like a baby, drifting in and out of consciousness to visits from The Gulldongs, Ronda and the filth. I'd answered some questions high on codeine and couldn't remember what answers I'd given. All I knew was that Paddy Hassle was in the clear and that Theo Oak was staring down the barrel of a life sentence.

"All in a day's work!" I bragged to a nurse who was in awe of me.

"Yes! Yes! You keep saying that Mr Hassle!" she left my room quickly, probably because she was blushing.

The time I had in bed to think, as well as the subsequent trial, revealed something however - something incredible and something I'd missed all along...

The dame - Mrs Stod.

She had played us all.

The truth was as follows:

John Stod had started frequenting Legs Thirteen from his office in town. He became immediately infatuated with the nameless woman. Mrs Stod - who turned out to be an ice-cold and calculated sociopath herself - saw the insecure and equally minted John Stod coming from a mile away. They were living together and then married in a short amount of time.

But there was trouble in paradise -

John Stod, though a talented music producer, was a shitty businessman. And everything started going tits-up financially.

When the dame caught whiff of this and sensed her lifestyle under threat, she went with a proposal to her boss at Legs Thirteen - none other than Theo Oak.

The proposal was to rip Stod off together.

A fifty-fifty split.

Oak acting as a helping hand, and the dame acting as a sleeper agent and saboteur.

To begin with, it worked. Oak greased Stod up good, and at home Mrs Stod got into his ear, telling him what a good opportunity it was for them both.

It was at this time, however, that a spanner found its way into the works... (Can you believe the prosecutor actually used that metaphor in court? He actually described me as a fucking spanner!) And that was none other than the good-looking, thick-fringed, best P.I. in town... Paddy fuckin' Hassle.

Mrs Stod fell for me. No doubt I was a safety net – a bit of muscle if things went sour with her husband and boss.

Foolishly (and most likely drunkenly), I had told her things about my past that she could have used against me. (Namely the *damsel in distress* issue. She knew if she played one, that I'd come running.)

But the dame got sloppy.

She was so cocky and full of herself at work, that one of the other girls told John Stod about her infidelities.

This caused trouble.

A heart-broken John Stod started ignoring Oak's phone calls, missing meetings, and getting cold feet. He was more concerned with his wandering lover than any financial problems he might have been facing.

Oak was pissed.

He'd wasted time and money on Stod, and the dame had fucked it all up.

So, he told her that not only was the split now *all* his, but if she valued her life then she had to continue working for him on the inside.

Infuriated, the dame started concocting her own scheme. A plot that would rip off *both men* and leave her with everything. And what was that?

Bugging Stod's office.

She recorded every single meeting between the men. The entirety of Stod's descent from fumbling businessman into white collar gangster was all on tape. Bribery, extortion, embezzlement, fraud, tax avoidance, so on and so on. She had enough material to bribe both men for the rest of their lives.

But the spanner was back again...

Stod had found my number on her phone and confronted her about it.

The dame, lying on her toes, told him that one of the girls at the club had given her the number. Paddy Hassle was a P.I. and she was going to pay him to track down an old friend.

The lie was good.

She thought she'd fooled him again.

What she hadn't counted on, however, was Stod coming to see me... coming to see me and asking me to investigate his own wife.

When I turned up at Legs Thirteen, I rumbled the chick. She felt threatened. She wanted me out of the picture. So, she paid a local lovesick thug to mug me, steal an advance I had foolishly told her about, and use it to buy and plant enough cannabis in my car to send me down and remove me for good.

But I was too smooth – like a petrol slick on the ocean – I bobbed and weaved her treachery like a sloppy jab.

So, she upped the stakes... all the way to murder.

When she first met Val Vulva, we'll never know. But she saw an opportunity in the hell-raising front man (who coincidentally also turned out to be a frequenter of Legs Thirteen, though he had spent some time on their barred list).

She knew Stod was flogging The Gulldongs to Oak, so she got into her boss's ear. She told him about Vulva and the liability he was – a threat to the band's success, thus Oak's investment.

His selfishness paired with his bloodlust soon blinded him. He decided Val Vulva had to be terminated in order to protect his new venture.

"Let's kill him!" he put the idea to Stod (unknowingly on tape, of course).

Stod was against it at first. Until one morning, when his beloved wife *broke down* and confessed to *two* affairs...

One, with the rock n' roll front man – Val Vulva.

And another, with the Irish P.I. – Paddy Hassle.

Distraught and enraged, Stod was suddenly in favour of not only butchering Val Vulva, but also framing the drunken mick as his killer.

The dame's espionage was paying off...

Only I was still to savvy. I evaded arrest. I was on the run. I was showing up here, showing up there, affecting business and proving to be more of a threat than any of them first imagined.

At this point, the cunning vixen decided to do a one-eighty –

She decided to help me, if only momentarily...

Rather than leave me to figure it all out, if she got herself involved and handed over evidence, she would not only get both men arrested, but also cover-up her own involvement. Stod and Oak would be in prison, and she would inherit all the assets.

She texted me before my suicide attempt.

She knew I'd hand over the evidence.

But she also knew that I'd sooner or later figure her out... hence I had to go too. So, she paid the lovesick thug to work her over, then she turned up at the pub, battered and bloody, knowing that I'd go straight after Stod and Oak, and straight into certain death.

And that was that.

I couldn't help but admire her.

If she'd been born rich in Solihull, rather than piss-poor in Ladywood, she'd have made one hell of a chess champion, businesswoman, or entrepreneur... She would have been on Dragon's Den, crossing and uncrossing those killer legs, while shooting down pitches with impunity.

In the end, after all the chaos at Stod's house, she stole what cash and jewellery she could and then disappeared in the Daimler.

The police had tracked it down to a garage in Manchester. She'd flogged it for cash under a false name and disappeared once more.

She hadn't won. But you couldn't really say that she'd lost.

A while later I was sat in Legs Thirteen. I'd refused the Holsten and asked for a Guinness. I'd drank enough Holsten in my life to drown a whale, and although the Guinness in there was shit, a badly poured Guinness was still better than the best lager on offer.

I put on *Miss Judy's Farm* by *Faces* on the jukebox. But when it ended some wanker put on *Borderline* by *Madonna*.

Bad as it was, it probably suited the place.

Legs Thirteen was strangely quiet.

I'd been at The Elizabeth before for a bit, but Apollo wasn't there. He'd taken a holiday back home to St Kitts and I didn't know if he'd return. Honestly, I wouldn't have blamed him.

I was watching the telly behind the bar and The Gulldongs were on MTV. They were going on as a three-piece. Patrice, loud-mouth and extrovert naturally, was the new singer. Their debut album was titled *Vulva*. The interviewer and wreck-head fans thought it was just a lewd rock n' roll joke, and The Gulldongs refused to comment... (He'd always be a part of them.)

Oak was in prison for life.

Stod was dead.

The bird was gone.

And I was out of work.

The Guinness tasted okay.

Only I think it tasted better as a wanted man. Each droplet could have been my last. But now I had time and a wallet. Freedom and I could drink as many as we liked. The appeal was gone.

"Fuck it," I said, deciding to go home.

I wondered about Mrs Stod for a second, as I pulled out some cash to cover the evening's tab.

Was it her degenerate upbringing that made her totally obsessed with wealth?

"Who cares," I put the cash down.

I knew she certainly didn't.

People go through their whole lives without ever really understanding why they do the things they do. And they're probably better off for it.

Just as I raised the final droplets of Guinness to my lips, I sensed someone walk up beside me. It was another customer, waiting to order a drink.

I finished and placed my glass down on the bar, beside the customer's hand. I stood up, and as I did, I looked at their hand...

There was a tattoo of a swallow on it.

I paused.

Then I sat back down on the stool.

*Play it cool, Hassle...*

In the mirror behind the bar, I looked up shyly. Beside me was a man, a rough looking cunt with a tattoo I recognised and a laugh that sounded familiar in my drunken ears. A laugh that brought me back to a night a while back, in an alley, bleeding and piss-soaked.

It was him. The final page unturned. The final bastard un-twatted.

Closure!

After the thug got served his brandy and coke, I demanded another Guinness.

I slammed it quickly, culchie style, and smelt my old man hovering somewhere nearby.

In the mirror, I watched the thug wander over to the men's room and continue inside.

He hadn't recognised me. So, I finished the Guinness and smiled. Then I gave Putlog a gentle pat underneath the sleeve of my new leather jacket.

"This is my life..." I told myself. "And it'll have to do."


I was Paddy Hassle.

The best fuckin' P.I. in town.

Printed in Great Britain
by Amazon

77122507R00135